Guiding his horse ~~forward slowly,~~ Longarm struck a match and held the lucifer's flame to the makeshift fuse. It caught right away. Without wasting any time, he heaved the jar toward the Hell Riders.

It exploded like a bomb, sending flames and shards of glass spraying through the night. Several of the Hell Riders were caught in the blast. Their horses screamed and reared and toppled. The raiders' dusters were on fire, and so were the hoods they wore. The Hell Riders shrieked as real flames wreathed their heads.

Longarm lit the fuse on another jar of the liquid hellfire and flung it among the raiders as Barstow and his men opened up their Winchesters and Colts. Their horses crashed into those of the Hell Riders. Mounts went down and men grappled hand to hand for their lives. Gun thunder filled the air, and the night sky was lit up by muzzle flashes like a lightning storm rolling across the prairie.

Longarm was in the thick of the fighting, his Colt bucking and roaring in his hand until the hammer fell on an empty chamber. He holstered it, pulled his Winchester from the saddle boot, and emptied it as well. One of the Hell Riders loomed close beside him, shouting obscene, hate-filled curses as he swung his gun toward the big lawman. Longarm lashed out one-handed with the rifle, smashing the barrel across the face of the flowing hood. The Hell Rider went backward out of his saddle, his yell cut off by the slashing hooves of another horse as it trampled him.

◆━━━◆ TABOR EVANS ◆━━━◆

LONGARM

AND THE HELL RIDERS

JOVE BOOKS, NEW YORK

THE BERKLEY PUBLISHING GROUP
Published by the Penguin Group
Penguin Group (USA) Inc.
375 Hudson Street, New York, New York 10014, USA
Penguin Group (Canada), 90 Eglinton Avenue East, Suite 700, Toronto, Ontario M4P 2Y3, Canada
(a division of Pearson Penguin Canada Inc.)
Penguin Books Ltd., 80 Strand, London WC2R 0RL, England
Penguin Group Ireland, 25 St. Stephen's Green, Dublin 2, Ireland (a division of Penguin Books Ltd.)
Penguin Group (Australia), 250 Camberwell Road, Camberwell, Victoria 3124, Australia
(a division of Pearson Australia Group Pty. Ltd.)
Penguin Books India Pvt. Ltd., 11 Community Centre, Panchsheel Park, New Delhi—110 017, India
Penguin Group (NZ), 67 Apollo Drive, Rosedale, North Shore 0745, Auckland, New Zealand
(a division of Pearson New Zealand Ltd.)
Penguin Books (South Africa) (Pty.) Ltd., 24 Sturdee Avenue, Rosebank, Johannesburg 2196,
South Africa

Penguin Books Ltd., Registered Offices: 80 Strand, London WC2R 0RL, England

This is a work of fiction. Names, characters, places, and incidents either are the product of the author's imagination or are used fictitiously, and any resemblance to actual persons, living or dead, business establishments, events, or locales is entirely coincidental.

LONGARM AND THE HELL RIDERS

A Jove Book / published by arrangement with the author

PRINTING HISTORY
Jove edition / August 2007

ISBN: 978-0-515-14337-9

JOVE®
Jove Books are published by The Berkley Publishing Group,
a division of Penguin Group (USA) Inc.,
375 Hudson Street, New York, New York 10014.
JOVE is a registered trademark of Penguin Group (USA) Inc.
The "J" design is a trademark belonging to Penguin Group (USA) Inc.

PRINTED IN THE UNITED STATES OF AMERICA

10 9 8 7 6 5 4 3 2 1

Chapter 1

The man on the lunging bay twisted in the saddle to trigger the gun in his hand. Orange muzzle flashes stabbed through the darkness as the revolver blasted. The rider couldn't tell if he hit anything or not. He just wanted to slow down his pursuers if he could.

Sweat beaded his forehead as he faced forward again. The night wasn't that hot. It was fear that made the sweat pop out.

Fear of hot lead smashing into him. Fear of a hangman's noose choking out his life.

One of those fates awaited him if he was caught, sure as hell.

He jammed the gun back in its holster and leaned forward over the neck of the galloping horse to make himself a smaller target. He couldn't hear anything except the pounding of the animal's hooves on the hard-packed prairie and the slugging of his own heart.

His name was Matt O'Hara, and he was on the run from a crime he hadn't committed.

Well, actually, he *had* robbed the bank, or at least tried to—he couldn't deny that. But he hadn't had any choice; it was that or lose the horse ranch he had worked so hard to establish. All because that bastard Phelps wouldn't give him a little more time on his loan. And Phelps wouldn't have put the pressure on him if Matt still planned to marry the banker's daughter, Abigail.

Everything had been fine until Abby decided she didn't want to get married after all, at least not to Matt O'Hara. "I'm sorry," she had told him, but she hadn't sounded all that regretful. "I realize now that you're just not the love of my life, Matt." As if all the promises they had made to each other hadn't meant a damned thing.

So she had tossed him aside like he was nothing, and Phelps had said there wouldn't be any more extensions on the loan, and by God, Matt had to get his hands on the money some way, and the bank was sitting right there. . . .

Besides, it was justice, that's what it was, to rob the bank and then use the loot to pay back that money-grubbing skinflint. He would disguise himself so well that nobody would ever know who he was. Just a masked bandit who had gotten away with a couple thousand dollars.

That was the way it was *supposed* to work out, anyway.

Matt had waited until just before the bank was about to close for the day, when nobody was inside except for Josiah Phelps and the teller, Harvey Lapreste. Harvey was a mild little fella, and Matt didn't expect any trouble from him, especially after he shoved the barrel of a six-gun in his face.

"Put all the money from the cash drawer in that gunny-sack," he had growled, making his voice deeper and rougher than normal so that nobody would recognize it. Harvey had reached for the sack, perfectly willing to do as he was told.

But then Marshal Chad Haimes had wandered into the bank unexpectedly, and Harvey had lunged across the counter and grabbed Matt's mask, pulling it down and knocking his hat off at the same time, and Matt was so startled that he pulled the trigger without even thinking about what he was doing.

The shot was powerfully loud, so loud it hurt his ears, and Harvey Lapreste was flung backward with blood on his white shirt and a surprised look on his face. Marshal Haimes hauled out his old long-barreled Remington and started blasting away with it. Matt vaulted the counter, nearly tripped on Harvey's sprawled body, and used the gun to swat Phelps out of the way as he lit a shuck for the bank's back door.

He hated to admit it, but it had felt mighty good to clout the sour-faced old bastard.

With bullets flying around his head, he'd made it out the back, dashed along the alley, and grabbed the first horse he could find, the long-legged bay that was galloping along under him now. That made him a horse thief as well as a bank robber and murderer, he supposed. He had left his own horse in front of the bank, but there was no way he could have reached it, of course. Not with Chad Haimes standing in the doorway shooting at him.

In the hours since then, as he fled west across the Kansas prairie, Matt had tried to figure out some way he could get out of this unholy mess. But there just wasn't one. Even if he had killed Harvey Lapreste—and poor Harvey had sure as hell *looked* dead when he went down— Phelps had seen Matt's face, and Marshal Haimes probably had, too. And his horse was tied up right outside, for God's sake!

Matt was forced to conclude that he wasn't nearly as smart as he'd thought he was, and desperation had made him even stupider. In the space of a few short hours he had gone from being a poor but honest rancher to facing the rest of his life as a fugitive, a wanted outlaw and killer.

And to top it all off, he hadn't gotten any money from the bank. Not one red cent.

Yeah, he was some desperado, all right.

Chad Haimes had rounded up a posse in a hurry and come after him. Matt had a bit of a lead, but the horse he had stolen wasn't the fastest in the world, and as the light of day faded, the posse had begun to whittle down the gap and draw within rifle range. Matt saw puffs of dust off to both sides of him and knew they came from bullets striking the ground.

Luckily—the first bit of luck he'd had all day, in fact—darkness soon fell and the posse stopped wasting lead. They were still back there behind him, though. Matt was sure of it. He turned and blazed away at them from time to time, just to keep them from getting too close.

He didn't know where he was anymore. Miles and miles of prairie had flashed past beneath the horse's hooves. All he knew for certain was that he was somewhere west of the town where he had begun his career of outlawry. He had fled in that direction, and he was pretty sure he hadn't gotten turned around.

But the way things had been going today, he might be wrong about that, he realized. What if he had gone in a big circle and was even now heading right back where he had come from? Right back to a bunch of folks who would like nothing better than to string him up from the nearest cottonwood tree . . .

He hauled back on the bay's reins, slowing the horse to a walk. He had to study the stars and try to orient himself, figure out as close as he could just where he was. Maybe the posse was still far enough behind him that he could afford to do that.

The horse stopped on its own. Matt had been running the animal for quite a while, never daring to slow down much and certainly not to stop so that the horse could have a proper blow. He was a little surprised the poor varmint hadn't collapsed before now.

But that didn't mean he could afford to take pity on his stolen mount. He nudged the horse with his knees and said, "Come on, let's go."

The horse just stood there, its sides heaving.

Matt felt panic welling up inside him. If he didn't get moving, the posse would catch up to him. Maybe if he walked the horse for a short distance, it would recover enough to carry him again. He swung down from the saddle and started tugging on the reins.

"Come on, horse. Come on, damn it."

Something was wrong. Matt stiffened and frowned, first in alarm, then in puzzlement as he realized that the night was utterly quiet. No sound of galloping hoofbeats came to his ears. If the posse was still on his trail, wouldn't he have heard their horses?

As he asked himself that question, understanding struck him almost like a physical blow. He couldn't hear the posse because the posse wasn't back there anymore. Sometime after darkness had fallen, they had given up. That meant he had been turning around and shooting at . . . nothing.

Luck had been with him after all. In fact, he had been so lucky that thinking about it made his knees weak. The shots he had squeezed off from time to time could have acted as a beacon to those following him. If they had been a little more stubborn about catching him, they would have seen his muzzle flashes and could have tracked him by them.

As it was, though, he had given his pursuers the slip. He still faced a life of running from the law, of never being able to return to his ranch, of always having to keep an eye out over his shoulder for trouble sneaking up behind him.

But that was a whole hell of a lot better than figuring he wouldn't live to see the sun rise the next morning.

Reaction caught up with him, made him stop pulling on the reins and lean against the horse's shoulder instead. The animal's hide was covered with sweaty foam, but Matt didn't care. The relief that filled him was so powerful he could barely stand up.

For long moments he waited there like that, listening to the quiet, feeling the frenzied hammering of his pulse slow to a calmer rhythm. At last he took a deep breath and said, as much to himself as to the horse, "All right, we've got to keep moving. Just because they ain't on my trail right now doesn't mean they won't be again later."

It was possible that Marshal Haimes and the men he had deputized to ride with him had just stopped and made camp for the night. Come morning, they might try to pick up Matt's trail and follow him. Because of that, Matt had to put as much distance as he could between him and them.

He looked up at the glittering stars. As far back as he could remember, he had been one to gaze at the stars, and his pa had taught him how to steer by them. Matt was convinced he was still heading west. Colorado was in that direction. He wasn't sure how far off it was, but maybe once he reached the border, he would be safe. No posse would chase him clear into another state, he told himself.

The bay had rested enough so that it took a grudging step when Matt tugged on the reins, then another and another. Man and horse trudged across the prairie, through the darkness, toward what Matt hoped would be safety.

A few hundred yards farther on, as they topped one of the small rises that undulated across this part of Kansas, Matt saw a light.

He stopped in his tracks, unsure of what to do next. The light probably came from some sodbuster's shanty. Matt could get food and water there, maybe some grain for the horse. He might have to take those things at the point of a gun, but if that was what he had to do, then so be it. He was an outlaw now, after all.

On the other hand, he thought as he scraped a hand over the beard stubble on his jaw, stopping at that farm meant he would be leaving witnesses behind who could put the posse right back on his trail.

Unless, of course, he didn't leave anyone alive.

His stomach clenched at the thought. Despite the fact that he had gunned down Harvey Lapreste, he wasn't a murderer. In fact, he'd liked Harvey and felt sick every time he thought about shooting him. So that was out. If he stopped at the farm, he would just have to take a chance on it maybe coming back to haunt him.

Better that than being haunted by the ghosts of innocent victims.

Or he could just circle around the place and go on. But he had been too nervous to eat lunch before carrying out the bank robbery, and he'd been on the run ever since, so he hadn't had anything to eat since breakfast and his stomach was mighty empty. Even a cold, stale biscuit would be good right now.

Life was full of risks, he thought. "Let's go," he said to the horse, and they walked toward the light.

He hadn't gone very far before he heard the swift rataplan of hoofbeats. The sound made him curse and reach for the gun on his hip. That damned posse was back!

Matt realized an instant later that the hurrying riders were ahead of him, not behind. He supposed it was possible that the members of the posse could have gotten past him somehow in the darkness, but it didn't seem very likely. Until about a quarter of an hour earlier, he had been moving as fast as he could across the plains, and he'd been well ahead of the posse when he started his flight.

It was somebody else, then, riding through the night toward some unknown destination. Nothing to do with him. He decided he would stay where he was until the hoofbeats faded away and the riders were gone. Then he would pay a visit to that farm and beg some supper from whoever lived there before moving on.

Matt's nerves were stretched tight as that newfangled barbed wire he had seen advertised. He waited impatiently for the group of riders to pass on out of hearing. Instead, the hoofbeats stopped short. Matt frowned. Maybe the riders had gotten where they were going. Maybe there was another farm or ranch nearby. Sound could travel for a long way out here on the prairie. The riders might not have been that close to him to start with. He sighed and started walking toward the yellow glow again.

As he came closer, he was able to make out more details and saw that his guess had been correct. He saw a squat dwelling constructed of blocks of sod carved out of the land. There were no windows in a house like that, so the light had to be coming through an open door. He saw a pole corral off to one side with the dark shapes of several animals inside it. Milk cows, maybe, or mules that the sodbuster used to pull his plow.

He opened his mouth to howdy the house. Nighttime visitors who didn't call out first were likely to be greeted with buckshot or rifle fire. But before he could say anything, somebody let out a strident yell and hoofbeats once again thundered through the night, practically on top of him this time. He twisted around and clawed for his gun as a horde of startling apparitions burst from the darkness and bore down on the sod shack, howling like banshees out of Hades as guns roared and Colt flame bloomed red in the night.

Banshees from hell was just about right, Matt thought wildly as he jerked his gun up, because the riders who were about to trample him. . . .

Their heads were on fire.

Chapter 2

He was only human, after all, thought Longarm as he watched the blonde's head bob up and down over his groin. Any fella would be a mite distracted under these circumstances. He tried not to groan as the gal's warm, expert tongue slid along the underside of his shaft.

Her name was Melissa, or at least that's what she had told him. With a soiled dove it was hard to be sure she was telling the truth about much of anything. Gals like her, their stock in trade was every bit as much telling an hombre what they thought he wanted to hear as it was their bodies.

As if to prove that point, Melissa lifted her head and gasped, then said, "My God, Custis, you're so big you just wear out a girl's mouth. I reckon I could lick this thing all night and not cover all of it." She gave him an impish smile. "Why don't we find out?"

"Maybe later," Longarm told her as he reached down to lightly grasp her shoulders and urge her up. "Right now I got something else in mind."

"I like the sound of that," she said, purring like a kitten as she straddled him. He was sitting with his back propped against the headboard of the bed in the room where she had brought him, upstairs in this little settlement's only saloon.

She planted her knees on either side of his hips and moved so that the tip of his manhood teased the wet folds between her legs.

They were both naked as jaybirds, having undressed each other with plenty of kissing and caressing and fondling along the way. She cupped her breasts, lifting and squeezing them so that the hard brown nipples pointed at Longarm's face like the barrels of two tiny guns. "Suck them, Custis," she said with a pleading note in her voice.

Longarm obliged, drawing each of the pebbled rings of woman flesh between his lips in turn. While he was sucking one nipple he played with the other one, strumming the hard bud with his thumb. Melissa lowered her head so that the thick blond hair hung around her face, and she gave little panting moans of pleasure. Those noises became more genuine when Longarm slipped his other hand between their bodies and squeezed her mound. His thumb moved rapidly over the sensitive nubbin at the top of her opening. She was actually getting worked up now.

"Damn you, Custis," she groaned. With a downward thrust of her hips, she impaled herself on him, sheathing his shaft all the way inside her heated, clasping femininity.

Nature had indeed been generous in Longarm's endowment. It was long and thick and right now rock-hard as Melissa bounced up and down on it. She wrapped her arms around Longarm's neck and mashed her mouth against his. Her sweet lips were open and he accepted the invitation, thrusting his tongue between them to engage in a sensuous dance with her tongue. He put his arms around her to draw her even tighter against him. Her apple-shaped breasts flattened against his broad, muscular chest.

She rode him like she was trying to gallop home to the finish line in a high-stakes race. After a few minutes she tore her mouth away from his and panted. "Deeper! Deeper!" Longarm didn't figure he could get much deeper—he was pretty much bottoming out with every

10

stroke—but he did the best he could, and somehow he delved into depths he hadn't reached before. Melissa threw her head back, cords standing out in her neck and a grimace of pure pleasure stretching her lips away from her teeth as shudders and spasms of culmination began to roll through her, and that sight pushed Longarm right over the edge. His own climax gushed forth, filling her with a scalding flood. Their juices mixed and overflowed, soaking them both.

Once she had peaked, Melissa sagged against him, resting her head on his shoulder as she drew in deep, satisfied breaths. Longarm stroked her hair and her back. He nuzzled his lips against her ear. . . .

And whispered, "Where's Dog McCluskey?"

She jerked back, trying to twist out of his arms and reach for the little table beside the bed where he had coiled his gun belt. He pulled her away before she could get her hands on the walnut butt of the Colt that stuck up from the holster. She opened her mouth wide and Longarm tried to get a hand over it before she could make a sound, but he wasn't quite quick enough. She screamed, "Feeney!"

Longarm threw her out of the bed, flinging her one way while he went the other. His fingers had just closed around the gun butt when the door crashed open and the big red-headed Irishman who worked behind the bar downstairs came roaring through it like an avalanche. He had a bungstarter in one hand and a sawed-off shotgun in the other. Longarm rolled off the bed as the shotgun exploded and blew a big hole in the mattress where he had been a heartbeat earlier. Feathers flew in the air, filling it like snow. That was better than blood and guts splashing everywhere, Longarm thought.

Longarm hit the floor hard but hung on to the gun. He snapped a shot at Feeney's legs, hoping to knock the man off his feet. The bullet missed, though, and Feeney swung the bungstarter with wicked speed. It smacked the Colt right out of Longarm's fingers and the impact numbed his whole hand, to boot.

For a second, Longarm wondered if Feeney had fired both barrels of the sawed-off, or just one. If it was just one, he was about to get his brains splattered all over the room. He pulled his feet under him and surged up off the floor anyway, meeting Feeney's attack with a diving tackle. The bungstarter whipped through the air above Longarm's head, missing him. Longarm slammed into the bartender and wrapped his arms around Feeney's thighs. Feeney was a big gent, but Longarm was no lightweight himself. With a startled yell, Feeney went over backward.

He landed on the floor with a crash like a giant redwood toppling in the forest. That knocked the breath out of him and kept him still long enough for Longarm to club his hands together and bring them down as hard as he could in the middle of Feeney's face. The big nose over the sweeping red handlebar mustache pulped under the impact. Feeney howled in pain as blood spurted. Longarm lifted his fists and smashed them down again. He wanted to finish this as fast as he could. He hated fighting naked.

A gun blasted and plaster showered down around Longarm, telling him that the shot had been directed toward the ceiling. The next one probably wouldn't be, though, and Melissa confirmed that by yelling, "Stop it! Stop it or I'll kill you!"

Feeney was stunned and out of the fight for a few minutes, anyway. He had dropped the bungstarter and the shotgun, but Longarm didn't reach for either of the weapons. Instead he looked up at Melissa, who was pointing his own gun at him, and said, "Be careful, gal. That smokepole doesn't have a hair trigger, but it don't take much to make it go off."

"I know, damn you. I ought to shoot you anyway, for what you did . . . screwin' me when all you really wanted to do was find Dog McCluskey! I'll bet you're a damn lawman!"

Longarm sighed. All he had told her earlier was that his name was Custis, never mentioning that the full handle was Custis Long or the fact that he was a deputy United States marshal working out of the Denver office. He supposed that question about McCluskey was a dead giveaway, though, since the Dog was well-known to be an owlhoot wanted by federal, state, and, no doubt, local authorities.

"I'm a deputy U.S. marshal," Longarm admitted now, "so you don't want to go shooting me. That'll get you into all sorts of trouble you don't want to be in, Melissa."

She glared at him. "You just let me be the judge of that. Feeney told me there was something wrong about you. He had you figured for a bounty hunter. He said he'd be right outside the door if you tried anything funny."

Longarm glanced down at the Irishman, who was making noises and blowing bubbles in the blood that had run down from his ruined nose over his mouth. When he looked up at Melissa, he said, "The Dog must have paid you pretty good to see to it that nobody got on his trail."

She sneered. "Dog didn't have to pay us. He's our friend. He takes good care of us."

Longarm suppressed the urge to sigh. That was usually the way it went. Most outlaws were pretty smart about making people believe they were really on the side of the common folks. Hell, nobody cared all that much about banks and railroads except the rich men who owned them, right? Spend a little money, kiss all the gals, slap the fellas on the back and give 'em a *see*gar . . . that was all it took to make folks think you were some sort of hero, when all you really were was a cold-blooded, no-account outlaw who didn't give a damn about anybody but himself. Longarm had corraled enough varmints just like Dog McCluskey to know exactly what sort of man he was.

But Melissa didn't know, and she was the one who had the gun. Looked pretty good standing there pointing it at him, too, without a stitch on and her breasts heaving that way. Longarm stood up, slow and careful so she wouldn't get trigger-happy, and said, "I'm sorry for deceiving you. I thought maybe if I could take you by surprise, you might blurt out what you know about the Dog."

"So you . . . you think that makes it all right for you to . . . to make me feel the way you did?" The barrel of the Colt shook, but not enough so that he wanted to take a chance on jumping her. What looked like honest-to-goodness tears welled up in her eyes and ran down her cheeks as she went on, "To make me forget for a minute that I'm nothin' but a whore?"

Now Longarm was starting to feel a mite bad about his behavior. He had hoped to trick her, sure, but he hadn't meant to hurt her feelings.

"I have a job to do," he said. "I got to find McCluskey and bring him in."

"Go to hell."

The flat, hard tone of voice told him that he didn't have any choice. He leaped forward, flying across the foot of the bed, as Melissa pulled the trigger.

The Colt boomed. Longarm felt as much as heard the wind-rip of the bullet beside his ear. Then he crashed into her and drove her back against the wall. Her head bounced hard off the plaster. She crumpled in his arms and dropped the gun.

"Son of a bitch," Longarm muttered as he lowered her to the bed, being as gentle and careful as he could. He hoped he hadn't killed her. Her eyelids fluttered, though, and her chest rose and fell steadily. She was just knocked out, and he was relieved to realize that.

Nobody else had shown up in the open doorway of the room. He wasn't too surprised by that. This little settlement in far western Kansas, just over the Colorado line, wasn't much more than a wide place in the road. Probably wasn't any law here, and the citizens knew how to mind their own business. They might be curious about the shots, but they weren't going to come investigate them, at least not until some time had passed.

While Feeney was still only half-conscious, Longarm rolled him onto his face, pulled the man's belt off, and used it to tie his hands behind his back. He ripped strips off the bedsheet and bound Melissa's wrists and ankles so that she couldn't make another grab for the gun. Then he got dressed while the two of them were regaining their senses.

He wore range clothes, which he knew made him look like a drifting cowhand—or a bounty hunter, as Feeney had suspected. Under the influence of Lemonade Lucy, the wife of President Rutherford B. Hayes, the Justice Department had issued guidelines saying that its employees, including deputy marshals, should be neatly dressed at all times, and that meant wearing a brown tweed suit, a vest, a white shirt, and a string tie. Longarm didn't mind sporting that garb in Denver—ladies liked a sharp-dressed man, after all—but out on the trail it was a pain in the butt and he tended to wear what he wanted to. Since he was the best deputy that Chief Marshal Billy Vail had and got more results than any of the others, Vail tended to look the other way most of the time when it came to Longarm's habits. That was why he put up with the drinking and the gambling and the womanizing and the getting to work late.

Because when it came to tracking down owlhoots, not many men were better than Custis Long.

He sat down on the edge of the bed to wait. Feeney regained consciousness first and started yelling and thrashing around. He could still move his legs even though his hands were tied. He didn't quiet down until Longarm put the muzzle of the Colt against his head behind his left ear.

"Don't kill me, mister," Feeney said. "For God's sake, don't kill me."

"Don't worry, old son," Longarm told him. "I ain't the sort to blow a man's brains out for no reason. So don't give me one."

"Whatever you want," Feeney said. "You a bounty hunter? There's some cash downstairs. You can take it."

"Deputy U.S. marshal."

"Oh." Feeney paused. "You can still take the money if you want. Just don't kill me."

"I don't want your money. I'm looking for Dog Mc-Cluskey."

From the bed, Melissa said, "Don't tell him, Feeney. Don't tell the son of a bitch a damned thing."

Longarm hadn't noticed that she was awake again. She must have been shamming. He said, "Hush up. I'm talking to Feeney."

Melissa ignored his order to be quiet. "Anyway, we don't know where the Dog is, do we, Feeney?"

"No, we don't," Feeney agreed. "And that's the truth, mister. Swear to God."

"He was here, though, wasn't he?"

"If you've been following him, you know his trail led here," Melissa replied. "He didn't tell us where he was going when he left, though."

"Which direction was he headed?"

"South."

"I thought it was north," Feeney said. "You sure he didn't say— Oh, hell."

Longarm prodded a little harder with the gun barrel. "So McCluskey told you what to say if anybody came looking for him, did he?"

"Feeney, you're the damn dumbest—" Melissa broke off with an exasperated sigh. "All right. He actually did go north. That's the gospel truth, Custis. I mean Marshal."

"You can still call me Custis," Longarm told her.

"Go to hell."

Longarm stood up and holstered the Colt. "Nope, I'm

16

going after McCluskey. With any luck it won't turn out to be the same thing."

"You're not going to ride off and leave us tied up like this, are you?"

"It won't take you too long to work yourselves loose. I don't reckon you'll starve to death in that amount of time. Anyway, as soon as I'm gone you can start hollering for help."

"What if we holler now?" Melissa asked with a defiant look on her face.

"Well, I can gag you, or just knock you both out again." Longarm shrugged. "It don't matter much to me."

"We'll be quiet, Marshal," Feeney said. "You just go on. We're mighty sorry about the trouble we caused you."

"Speak for yourself, you big dumb Mick," Melissa said.

"Aw, hell, you shouldn't ought to talk to me that way."

"I'll talk to you any way I want. If this damn lawman catches the Dog because of you, I'll . . . I'll . . ."

"I don't know why you feel that way about him," Feeney said in a sullen voice. "I treat you better'n he does."

"My God, you just run a saloon and a whorehouse! The Dog is . . . is . . . dashing!"

Longarm shook his head and left them there arguing. If he lived to be a hundred—a chancy proposition in his line of work—he'd never understand how some people could think the way they did. There was nothing dashing about being an owlhoot.

He went downstairs. The hour was late, and the saloon was empty. The cowhands who had been drinking there earlier must have all ridden back to their ranches. Longarm pushed through the batwings and stepped out onto the porch.

He was surprised to see a boy about eight years old sitting on the steps, petting a scruffy yellow tabby with battle-scarred ears. The boy had bright red hair, and when he looked up at Longarm, the big lawman saw that his face was covered with freckles.

17

"What are you doing sitting in front of a saloon at this time of night, younker?"

The boy stopped petting the cat long enough to say, "Waitin' for my ma and pa."

"Where are they?"

The boy jerked a thumb over his shoulder toward the saloon.

"Oh," Longarm said. "Your last name Feeney?"

"Yep."

"And your ma's got pretty blond hair?"

"Yep."

Longarm took a cheroot out of his pocket and clamped his teeth on it, leaving it unlit. Now that he'd made the acquaintance of this youngster, he felt sort of bad about busting his pa's nose and screwing his ma. But of course it wasn't the first time either of those things had happened to Feeney and Melissa. Probably wouldn't be the last, either.

"Like cats, do you?" Longarm asked around the cheroot.

"Sure."

"I'm looking for a dog, myself. Dog McCluskey."

"I know him. He's an outlaw."

"You didn't happen to see him ride out earlier today, did you?"

"Yep."

"Can you tell me which way he went?"

The boy pointed to the east.

"I'm obliged," Longarm said. He believed the boy more than he did either of the youngster's parents. He went down the steps and over to the hitching rail where his horse was tied. He pulled the reins loose and then paused with them in his hand before mounting up. "You know why they call him the Dog?"

For the first time the boy's eyes lit up with what appeared to be real interest. "No, why?"

Longarm grinned and said, "Because he's got a tail."

Chapter 3

Matt O'Hara squeezed the trigger and threw himself aside as the gun bucked in his hand. He hit the ground and rolled, expecting at any second to feel the slashing hooves of the horses cutting him to ribbons. The earth shook under him as if primordial leviathans were tromping by.

Then the riders, a dozen or more of them, were past him, and he was still alive after all, much to his surprise. Gasping from shock and breathlessness, he lifted his head and looked after the . . . the . . . whatever the hell they were.

They looked like men in long dusters, except for those blazing heads. They didn't wear hats, of course. Stetsons would have just burned up in the flames, Matt thought, then realized how bizarre it was that he could reach a logical conclusion like that when the subject was men whose heads were on fire.

Shots continued to ring out as Matt pushed himself onto hands and knees and then staggered to his feet. He had managed to hold on to his gun. He lifted it as he watched the riders attack the sodbuster's shanty. The sod shack was dark now, the lamp inside having been blown out or maybe shot out. A shotgun boomed from the doorway, followed by the cracking of a pistol.

Matt had always been one to stick up for the underdog, since he fit that description himself. And those bastards had come close to trampling him, which he didn't like. On top of the bad day he'd already had, it was just too much.

He started squeezing off shots, emptying his revolver at the raiders.

He wasn't sure if any of them had even noticed him when they almost rode him down, but they paid attention when he started shooting at them, all right. Several of the men whirled their mounts and charged back at him. Cold fear clamped fingers around his stomach as he got a good look at the terrible figures bearing down on him. When the hammer of his gun clicked on an empty chamber, he looked around for his horse. The bay was gone, though. It must have spooked and run off when the commotion started.

Matt couldn't blame the horse. What was happening here was enough to spook anybody.

He rammed his empty Colt in its holster and ran, darting sideways in an attempt to get out of the path of the riders. They just veered after him, though. The hoofbeats grew deafening behind him. The pursuers were close enough they could have riddled him with bullets, but clearly they wanted to trample him instead.

A dark line on the ground ahead of him caught his attention. It was a shallow gully snaking its way across the prairie, he realized as he came closer. It probably ran full of water during the occasional cloudburst. But it hadn't rained in these parts for a while, so the gully would be dry now. Matt plunged into it in a desperate dive.

Just in time, too, because in another moment he would have fallen under the hooves of the horses. The impact as he hit the bottom of the gully knocked the wind out of him. The horses were going too fast to stop, so they leaped over the little depression in the earth. Matt buried his face in the dirt, hoping he was low enough to avoid any flashing hooves.

He heard the flame-headed demons cursing as they tried to rein in their mounts. They cussed just like men. Matt punched cartridges from the loops on his shell belt and thumbed them into the Colt as he rolled over onto his belly. When he lifted his head, he saw the three riders turning their mounts to make another run at him. He brought the Colt up and triggered several times, not knowing if bullets would do any good against denizens of hell.

One of the riders yelled and toppled out of his saddle.

The varmint Matt had shot was the one closest to him. He scrambled out of the gully and lunged for the trailing reins of the horse with the empty saddle. Bullets whined around him as he grabbed the reins and the horn and swung up into leather. Bending low, he emptied the Colt to give himself some time and lunged away from there, spurring the horse he had grabbed into a gallop.

More shots rang out behind him. A giant fist crashed into his side. Matt cried out in pain and slumped forward, dropping his gun. His fingers tangled in the horse's mane as he struggled to keep himself from falling. He stayed in the saddle and guided the horse with his knees as the animal leaped the gully again and then headed for the sodbuster's shanty.

Matt's left side was numb. He knew he was hit bad. It shouldn't come as a surprise, he told himself. He had been shot at so many times today it made sense one of the slugs would get him sooner or later. Maybe dying wouldn't be too bad.

A core of stubbornness still flickered inside him, driving him on. Some unknowable something made him want to reach that soddy. The riders seemed to be breaking off their attack. Whoever was inside the shack must have put up too much of a fight.

Nobody shot at Matt as he rode through the crowd. They must have been unable to tell if he was one of them. They should have known he wasn't, because his head wasn't on fire. But he would take any break he could get, and suddenly he was through the ring of flame-headed gunslammers. He rode hard toward the shack.

So, naturally, the folks in *there* started shooting at him.

He felt the horse underneath him shudder as a bullet drove into its chest. The animal's galloping pace faltered, and then its front legs collapsed. Matt had just enough time to kick his feet free of the stirrups before he found himself flying through the air over the dying horse's head.

His momentum made him roll over several times when he hit the ground, bringing him that much closer to the shack. He was stunned, the breath having been knocked out of him yet again, and weakness from the loss of blood flooded through him. He wanted to jump and dive through the darkened but still-open doorway of the sod shanty, which was only a few yards away from him, but his muscles flat-out refused to work. All he could do was lie there gasping and hurting.

The shotgun boomed again from the shanty as one of the defenders tried to hurry the attackers on their way. A voice cried, "Get him and drag him in! I'll cover you!" A revolver blasted, again and again.

Matt felt hands grasping him a moment later. Someone started dragging him toward the door of the shack. He didn't resist; he couldn't have even if he'd wanted to. He was doing well enough to hang on to consciousness.

Stars floated in the night sky above them. Those pinpricks of light were blotted out a second later, and the small part of his brain that still functioned realized that he had been pulled inside the shack. It was even darker in here than it had been outside. He yelled as someone drove a knee into his chest, pinning him to the ground. Pain exploded from the wound in his side.

A gun barrel prodded him under the chin, and the same voice that had called out earlier ordered, "Don't move, Mr. Hell Rider, or I'll blow your damn head off."

The odd thing about the voice, Matt realized, was that it was female. And its owner, whoever she was, had him mixed up with somebody else. Hell Rider, she had called him. She thought he was one of those bastards with the flaming skulls! Hell Riders was a good name for that bunch, but he wasn't one of them.

He might have tried to explain that to her if he hadn't passed out just then. His last thought was to wonder if he would wake up in the hell that had spawned those diabolical raiders.

The pain in his side told Matt he was still alive. He struggled up out of the black cavern that had swallowed him earlier. Slowly, he became aware of the absolute gloom being relieved by a faint glow that grew stronger as he swam through ebony waves toward it.

He groaned.

"Son of a gun's awake. Bring that lantern over here, girl."

This time the voice belonged to a man. It cracked and rasped with age.

The light became even brighter, and even though Matt's eyes were still closed, he winced against its glare. As he moved his head a little, he felt as if he had begun to loop and spin crazily. He thought he was going to be sick.

The feeling went away after a few seconds, and the chaos inside his skull began to settle down. He shifted enough to make himself aware that he was lying on a hard bunk. He had to take shallow breaths because there was some sort of constriction around his midsection. After another moment he realized that bandages had been wrapped around him and pulled tight.

At least his captors weren't going to let him bleed to

death from the wound in his side, he thought. But were they captors or saviors? They didn't know it because they thought he was one of the raiders, but they might well have saved his life by dragging him inside the sod shack.

The air was filled with the damp, musty smell of the earth that had been carved in blocks and used to construct this dwelling. Matt smelled the reek of coal oil, too, from the lantern that was casting its light on him. Another scent came to him, lighter and more delicate. Soap and some sort of tonic water, he decided.

That was a woman smell. She had to be leaning over him. He forced his eyes open to get a look at her.

The rounded face peering down at him was framed by long, thick brown hair. Her cheeks and nose were smudged from powder smoke. Her eyes were a darker shade of brown than her hair. Matt put her age around nineteen or twenty, and even though she was frowning at him, he thought she was mighty pretty.

"Yeah, he's awake, all right," the girl said. She glared at Matt and went on, "Don't get any funny ideas, mister. We got no use for your bunch. I'd just as soon shoot you as look at you."

Another face hove into view, this one belonging to a white-bearded old-timer. "He ain't gonna try anything," the old man said. "He's too banged up to do nothin' but lay there."

The girl straightened. "Yeah, well, I don't trust him, Pap." She held the lantern in one hand and a six-gun in the other. A man's shirt and canvas trousers hugged the lines of her body. "I don't trust anybody who rides for Carlton Barstow."

"We don't know them Hell Riders work for Barstow," the old man said as if he were reminding her of something. "This is the first time anybody's even laid hands on one o' the polecats."

"Who else could be behind the trouble?" the girl demanded. "You know he's said all along he's going to run all the homesteaders out of this part of the country."

The old man nodded. "I know, I know. And you're prob'ly right. I'm just sayin' we need to try to get this fella to talk. I want to know how they manage to set their heads on fire like that and still ride around causin' trouble for folks."

Matt wouldn't have minded knowing that himself. He poked his tongue out, ran it over dry lips, and husked, "I . . . I'll talk."

The girl looked surprised. "He heard us."

"O' course he heard us. He was layin' right there awake."

The girl set the lantern aside and then pointed the gun at Matt's face. She held it with both hands and looped a thumb over the hammer.

"Talk, you son of a bitch," she ordered.

"Dadgum it, Claire, I've told you about that cussin'," the old-timer said. "Your ma would be plumb upset to hear the kind o' mouth you got on you."

"We can worry about my cussin' later," she snapped. "Right now we got a prisoner to question."

Matt said, "Well, if you'll just . . . shut up . . . I'll tell you . . . who I am."

The girl's face darkened. "Did you just tell me to shut up?"

Matt figured it wasn't going to do any good to argue with her. He ignored her and looked at the old man instead. "My name is . . . Matt O'Hara," he got out. "I'm not one of . . . the men who were . . . attacking you."

"You were with them," Claire insisted. "Where's your flaming head?"

"I saw your light," Matt went on as if she hadn't spoken. "I was coming in . . . about to holler . . . when those hombres rode up . . . and started shooting. . . . They almost . . . rode me down. . . . Made me mad . . . so I threw some lead at them."

The old man nodded. "I thought I seen somebody takin' a few potshots at them, even though it didn't make no sense to me at the time."

"Don't tell me you believe him!" Claire said.

"I got no . . . reason to lie. My horse ran off . . . I shot one of them . . . out of the saddle . . . grabbed his horse . . . tried to make it here so I could help you . . . fight them off."

The old-timer frowned and tugged on his beard. "I reckon he could be tellin' the truth. The rest o' the bunch was wearin' dusters, and he didn't have one. Head weren't on fire, neither."

"Their heads aren't really on fire," Claire said.

"Sure looked like it," the old man said, and Matt had to agree with him. He had never seen anything quite so grotesque, or so frightening.

"It's a trick of some kind," Claire insisted, but Matt thought she didn't sound convinced of that even though she was the one making the argument. She pointed at him and added, "You can see for yourself that he's got a real head."

"But I'm not . . . one of them," Matt insisted.

"Where'd you come from?" the old man asked.

Matt hesitated. He didn't want to tell them that he had been on the run from a posse. For some reason he didn't want to admit that he had tried to rob a bank and had shot and maybe killed a fella who had never done him any harm.

"I'm just a drifting cowpoke," he said. His voice was stronger now. "I was coming from over east of here. My horse played out, so I was walking him when those men came along and nearly stampeded right over me. I don't know what happened to my horse."

The old man looked at the girl and nodded. "I think he's tellin' the truth." He leaned down and went on, "Matt, you said your name was?"

"That's right. Matt O'Hara." He'd already told them that much, so there was no point in lying about it now.

"And you shot one o' them Hell Riders?"

Matt gave a weak nod. "Yeah. I saw him fall off his horse."

"Then he could still be out there somewhere."

That was possible, but Matt doubted it. He suspected that the raiders had taken their fallen compadre with them when they broke off the attack and galloped back to wherever they came from.

"We can look for him in the morning," Claire said. "In the meantime, we'd better take turns standing guard over this one, just in case he tries to get away."

Matt was about as weak as a newborn kitten and couldn't get away if his life depended on it, but he figured she wouldn't believe him if he told her that. So he just lay back on the bunk and closed his eyes. He might as well get some rest while he had the chance. Marshal Haimes and the posse might show up in the morning and haul him back to face prison or a hang rope, depending on whether or not Harvey Lapreste was dead.

"All right," the old man said to Claire. "You go ahead and get some sleep. I'll wake you up later."

"No, I'll take the first watch," she said. "I'm not that tired, anyway. Getting shot at makes me all wide-awake for some reason."

As Matt lay there, he hoped that come morning he could convince her to believe him. He wasn't sure why it was important to him that a brown-haired girl with powder-smoke smudges on her face thought he was telling the truth, but it was.

He dozed off, thinking that she would probably clean up real nice.

Chapter 4

It was true. Dog McCluskey had a tail.

Folks didn't find out about it until he'd had a falling-out with a dance-hall gal in Fort Worth, a girl he had been friendly enough with so that she'd seen the thing with her own eyes. About three inches long and maybe an inch in diameter, it protruded from the base of his spine. When people asked her how she had first come to notice it, she said, "I was lookin' over his shoulder and caught a glimpse of it waggin' back and forth one day while he was screwin' me."

When word got back to McCluskey—who before that time had been known by his given name of Abner—he had returned to Fort Worth in a rage and gone looking for the dance-hall gal with a straight razor, threatening to cut her titties off. No one doubted he would have carried out the threat if he'd caught her, either, because McCluskey was already wanted for murder and was known to be a bad man.

The girl had managed to avoid McCluskey and get out of town before he could lay his hands on her, and Mc-Cluskey himself had been forced to light a shuck shortly thereafter to avoid being arrested by the city marshal, Longhaired Jim Courtright, who was well known to be a proficient shootist. Texas was getting a mite too hot for

McCluskey anyway, so he headed for New Mexico Territory, robbed banks in Albuquerque, Santa Fe, and Taos, held up a train in Raton, and then escaped through the Sangre de Cristos before cutting east into Kansas, where he had spent the past six months waylaying stagecoaches. Several of those coaches had been carrying the United States mail, so robbing them was a federal offense.

Which explained why Longarm had picked up McCluskey's trail and was now following him. A week earlier, in Billy Vail's office in the Denver federal building, the chief marshal had handed the job to his most trusted deputy.

"The Dog, eh?" Longarm had said as he sat in the red leather chair in front of Vail's desk, right foot cocked on left knee, puffing on a three-for-a-nickel cheroot and blowing smoke rings toward the banjo clock on the wall. "I've heard of him. The owlhoot with a tail."

"It's not a real tail," Vail had said. The pink-cheeked, mostly bald chief marshal looked more like somebody's kindly ol' grandpa than he did a lawman, but he had been a hell-roarer in his time, riding for the Texas Rangers and packing a sheriff's badge before becoming a United States marshal. "Well, I guess it is, come to think of it. One of those odd things that folks are sometimes born with, like an extra thumb or a third nipple. But it's not a long fuzzy tail like you'd see on a real dog."

Somehow, Longarm thought that might have gone without saying, but Vail had said it anyway.

"Scientist fella name of Darwin claims we all used to be monkeys," Longarm had drawled. "I read about it in a book at the library. Maybe there's some truth to it and McCluskey ought to be called Monk instead of Dog."

The sound that Vail's breath made as it hissed between his teeth reminded Longarm of a pot that was about to boil over. "I don't care what he's called, just bring him in so he'll stop holding up stagecoaches and messing with the United States mail."

That was putting it simply enough, and Longarm had been trying to follow Billy Vail's orders ever since.

After leaving the little settlement where he'd had the run-in with Melissa and Feeney, Longarm rode a couple of miles and then stopped to make camp next to a narrow, winding creek. A few cottonwoods squatted on the bank. He tied his horse to one of them and spread his bedroll in the thick shadows under the tree. Instinct would wake him if anyone came along and got too close to him.

He slept the sleep of the just—and the just-laid—and woke up early the next morning refreshed and not too stiff from sleeping on the ground. A pot of coffee and a pan of flapjacks and bacon made him feel even better. He cleaned up the camp and saddled his horse, then rode eastward, taking his time and studying the ground in hopes that he would pick up the Dog's tracks.

In the time he had been trailing McCluskey, he had already grown familiar with the horseshoe prints from the outlaw's mount. Most shoes had nicks and scratches that made their prints unique. Unfortunately, men on the dodge traded horses pretty often, so Longarm knew he couldn't count on being able to continue trailing McCluskey that way.

People who thought of Kansas as being flat and featureless had never been to this part of the state. Along the western reaches of the Smoky Hill River the terrain was more rugged. The hills that rose in this area couldn't be called mountains by any stretch of the imagination, but they were still a welcome relief from the plains farther east. This was ranching country, although the seemingly endless tide of farmers that had filled up the eastern half of the state had begun to flow westward into these parts, too.

Longarm knew that before too many years passed,

barbed wire would put in an appearance and the days of the open range would be over. He could live with that. He had spent some time cowboying when he first came west after the end of the Late Unpleasantness fifteen years earlier, but he knew that progress was inevitable. In the West, that was going to mean fences and farms, and there wasn't a darned thing anybody could do about it.

But that didn't mean nobody would try to stop it. He knew that, too, so he wasn't surprised when around mid-morning he spotted a group of riders coming toward him with their rifles drawn and cradled in their hands. Folks around here were just naturally suspicious of strangers.

The leather folder that contained his badge and bona fides was tucked away in his saddlebag, and he intended to keep it there as long as he could. As one of the riders hailed him, he reined in and sat there in the saddle with his hands resting on the horn in plain sight. He counted eight riders approaching him, all of them tough-looking. As they brought their mounts to a stop, one of the men asked, "Who are you, mister, and what are you doing on Boxed B Range?"

"Didn't know I was," Longarm replied with the air of a man who was just drifting along and not looking for trouble. "Who does the spread belong to?"

"Mr. Carlton Barstow," the spokesman for the group of riders said. His tone of voice made it clear he thought Longarm ought to know who he was talking about.

As a matter of fact, Longarm had never heard of Carlton Barstow before, but he nodded anyway, as if the man had just told him he was on a range belonging to Charles Goodnight or John Chisum or one of the other cattle barons who were known all across the West.

"Well, Mr. Barstow's got himself a mighty fine-looking ranch, and you can tell him I said so."

"You still ain't told us who you are," the hard-faced cowboy said.

"I'm just a fella riding across Mr. Barstow's ranch. Name of Custis Parker." It was a good alias. Longarm had used it before. He supposed he was fond of it because Parker was his middle name and he wasn't likely to forget it.

One of the other men spoke up. "You're not one of them damn sodbusters, are you?"

Longarm put a surprised expression on his face and made a vague gesture that encompassed his clothing and his saddle rig. "Do I *look* like a sodbuster to you, old son?" he asked. He leaned over and spat on the ground. "I've always figured a job you can't do from horseback is a job that ain't worth doing."

Several of the men relaxed. Longarm might be a stranger, but to their minds he was a stranger who had things in common with them, and therefore he wasn't as much of a threat.

Not the ramrod of the group, though. He still watched Longarm through eyes narrowed with suspicion. "Maybe you're not a plowman yourself," he said, "but you could be workin' for them. They been makin' noises about how they might bring in somebody to protect them. Somebody who's handy with a gun."

Longarm bit back a curse. He had heard enough now to know what was going on here. Carlton Barstow figured he was the big skookum he-wolf of these parts, and he didn't like it that settlers were moving in and taking up homesteads on land that Barstow considered his, even though he might not have any legal claim to it. Longarm had seen similar conflicts play out dozens of times, in places from Texas to Montana, and they always had several things in common.

They were bloody. They were brutal. They were stupidly futile.

And in the end the cattlemen lost, because the settlers had the law on their side. You could spend all day going 'round and 'round about whether or not the law was *right*, but it didn't matter. The government would send in the army to protect the settlers if necessary, and even the toughest ranch crew was no match for the army.

But before things reached that point, people usually had to die. Sometimes quite a few people.

Longarm didn't want any part of a range war. He just wanted to find Dog McCluskey and arrest him. Or kill the son of a bitch, if he had to, and haul his carcass back to Denver if that was feasible. Bury him or leave him for the buzzards if it wasn't.

Longarm told the spokesman for the group of Boxed B hands, "You've got me all wrong. I'm not a hired gun, and I don't know a damned thing about any trouble your boss has been having with the sodbusters or anybody else. I'm just riding from one yonder to another and looking for an hombre along the way."

"Who would that be?"

Longarm took a chance. "Name of McCluskey. Some folks call him the Dog."

That ruffled their fur again. The ramrod said, "Any friend of Dog McCluskey must be a no-good owlhoot, too, and not welcome on the Boxed B. You better keep movin', Parker."

"Didn't say I was a friend of his, just that I'm looking for him. You know the Dog, then?" Longarm prodded.

"Know of him, right enough. And nothin' good, neither."

"He around these parts anywhere?"

For a second Longarm didn't think the cowboy was going to answer him, but then the man said, "Last I heard he was in Greenwood, paradin' around and actin' high and mighty like he was Jesse James or some such, instead of just a second-rate desperado."

"Where's this Greenwood?" The name was vaguely familiar to Longarm, but he couldn't place it.

"Settlement about ten miles east of here, just the other

side of the valley where all those damn farmers are movin' in."

Longarm nodded, dipping the brim of his flat-crowned, snuff-brown Stetson. "I'm obliged for the information."

It was the cowboy's turn to spit. He did so and then said, "I didn't tell you because I wanted to help you out. I told you because I want you off this range, and I figured that'd be the quickest way to get you to move on."

"Either way, I appreciate it."

Longarm hitched his horse into motion and rode past the group of cowboys, all of whom followed his progress with baleful stares. It would have been easier to just pull out his badge and tell them that he was a star packer, but in the past he had often found it was to his advantage to keep his identity and his real business concealed from folks until he'd had a chance to look around and get the lay of the land. Time enough then to tell them who he really was.

He didn't look back, but he felt their gazes boring into his back for quite a ways. Their hostility didn't bother him. The problems between cattlemen and farmers in this part of Kansas weren't any of his business. They could fight their damn range war if they wanted to.

He was staying out of it.

Later that day, still heading east, Longarm came to a broad, shallow valley and started seeing cultivated fields instead of grassy pastures where cattle grazed. He had reached farming country.

Once, the grass on this prairie had been grazed upon by vast herds of buffalo, and the red men who hunted those shaggy behemoths had been lords of the plains. Now most of the buffalo that were left had migrated down to the Texas Panhandle, and the Indians were all on reservations. Their glorious victory a few years earlier over the Seventh Cavalry and the man they called Yellow Hair, Colonel

George Armstrong Custer, had been the beginning of the end for the Plains Tribes, a prime example of winning a battle but losing a war. From time to time a spasm of violence between red men and white still occurred, like the final twitchings of nerves in a corpse, but those outbreaks didn't change anything. The way of life that had once ruled the prairie was still dead.

Replacing the buffalo and the Indian were cattle and cowboys, and they had had their time of ascendance, too, although a shorter one because of the inexorable advance of civilization. Now, in place after place, the grass was being turned under as the soil was broken and the seeds of crops and progress were sown. Longarm rode across the valley, and when he passed the isolated homesteads, he gave friendly waves to the gaunt, rawboned, sunburned men who trudged along behind their plows and mules, and tipped his hat to the equally gaunt, rawboned, and sunburned women who often labored right alongside their husbands. There would be plenty of work to do on these farms, and from the looks of the crops, the labor wasn't very rewarding. In most places the plants appeared to be rather stunted and scraggly.

When the sun was straight overhead, Longarm paused to consider what to do next. He could ride on to Greenwood, or he could stop at one of the sod shanties and maybe buy a meal. He wasn't interested in the food as much as he was in whatever information he might pick up from the homesteaders. He decided to stop at the next farm he came to.

Before that could happen, he spotted a vehicle coming across the prairie toward him. It was a covered wagon, he noted as it drew closer—not a Conestoga such as the pioneers used with a high, arching canvas cover over the back, but rather a smaller vehicle with walls and a roof enclosing everything except the driver's seat. Longarm was reminded of gypsy wagons and medicine-show wagons he had seen

36

in the past. Unlike either of those, however, this vehicle was plain, not painted in gaudy colors or decorated with pictures or fancy lettering.

Two people perched on the driver's seat, a man and a woman. The man clutched the reins, handling the team of four horses that pulled the wagon. When Longarm was about fifty yards away, he reined in and moved his horse a little to one side, intending to sit there and let the folks on the wagon drive on past him. Maybe if they looked friendly, he would venture a question or two about Dog McCluskey and about the settlement of Greenwood.

Instead, with no warning, the gent pulled back hard on the reins and jerked the team to a halt. He grabbed up a stick of some sort that lay on the floorboards at his feet and leaped down from the wagon. Then, waving the stick over his head, he raced across the plains, yelling, "Great purple hairstreak! Great purple hairstreak!"

Chapter 5

Clearly, the hombre had gone mad. Longarm wondered for a moment if he ought to take out his Winchester and shoot him, as he would have a rabid animal. That would probably upset the lady still sitting on the wagon seat, he told himself, so he decided against it. She seemed to be taking her companion's sudden descent into lunacy quite calmly.

As the man continued dashing around in a frenzy, Longarm heeled his horse into motion and rode over to the wagon. He tugged on the brim of his Stetson and said, "Howdy, ma'am. You want me to catch that fella for you? I got a rope here, and I reckon I can dab a loop on him."

She was a blonde in her midtwenties, and mighty easy on the eyes. She frowned and asked, "Why in the world would I want you to do that, sir?"

"Well . . . he might hurt himself, running around like that all crazy-like."

She shook her head, causing the fair hair to swirl around her shoulders. "He's not crazy. He thought he saw a great purple hairstreak."

She didn't *look* touched in the head, Longarm thought, but maybe she was. She was spouting the same sort of gibberish as the fella with the stick, after all. Maybe they had both escaped from some sort of asylum. It was a damned shame to think of somebody as pretty as her not being right, but Longarm knew that such handicaps sometimes turned up in the oddest places.

"Is he afraid this, uh, great purple hairstreak is gonna hurt him?"

"Goodness, no! How could it hurt him? Unless of course he tripped and fell while pursuing it, or something like that."

"That's a good enough reason right there to round him up, I reckon—"

Longarm fell silent when he realized that the man had ceased darting hither and yon, as the old saying went, and was now on his way back to the wagon, trotting along in a spritely fashion with a big grin on his face. He was blond-haired like the woman, with muttonchop side-whiskers and a drooping mustache. He wore canvas pants, a work shirt, a broad-brimmed straw planter's hat, and high boots that laced up. He still carried the stick, and as he came closer, Longarm saw that there was some sort of net attached to the end of it.

"Hello, there," he greeted Longarm, then lifted the net, which he was holding closed with one hand. "I caught it, you know."

"A great purple hairstreak?" Longarm said.

The man's face lit up with a giddy grin. "You're familiar with *Atlides halesus*?"

"Sure." By now Longarm had noticed the bright blue and purple wings fluttering inside the net. "Butterfly, ain't it?"

"A grand, beautiful butterfly," the man agreed. "I can't wait to kill it and mount it."

Things were starting to make sense, sort of. The fella wasn't a lunatic after all. He was a butterfly collector. Longarm had heard of hombres like that, but he couldn't recall ever running into one before. Of course, some folks might say it was a little crazy for a grown man to go run-

40

ning around catching butterflies, but Longarm was willing to live and let live as long as nobody tried to throw a net over *his* head.

"So the great purple hairstreak is the name of that critter?" he said.

"Certainly. I thought you knew that."

"A fella's never too old to learn new things. My name's Custis Parker, by the way."

"I'm Roy Archer. This is my sister Guinevere."

"My mother liked the King Arthur stories," Guinevere Archer explained.

Longarm nodded. He had read some of those yarns about knights in armor and such. Fact of the matter was, he had once had a run-in with a no-good varmint who'd sported a suit of armor while holding up stagecoaches, down in the Four Corners country. So he knew who the original Guinevere was and knew that she was supposed to be very beautiful. This gal sure fit the description. And she was Archer's sister, not his wife. That was good to know.

"Are you a cowboy, Mr. Parker?" Roy Archer asked.

"Been known to work in that line," Longarm said. "Right now, though, I'm just drifting. Heading for Greenwood, in fact. You folks from there?"

"That's where we're staying at the moment, yes. We actually live in Philadelphia, though."

"You came all the way out here to, uh, chase butterflies, did you?"

"The pursuit of lepidoptera is both my profession and my passion. It's a lucky man who can combine those two things, isn't it?"

Longarm couldn't argue with that. In fact, he wasn't sure he could argue about anything with Archer, since the man still acted like he'd been out in the sun a mite too long.

"Yeah," Longarm said. "You happen to know if a man named McCluskey is still in Greenwood?"

"The famous desperado?" Guinevere asked.

"You've heard of Dog McCluskey?"

"Oh, yes. People in the settlement talk about him quite a bit. I gather that he's the most famous person to ever visit Greenwood."

That just showed what a backwater burg Greenwood was, Longarm thought, when the folks who lived there got excited about having an outlaw like Dog McCluskey in their midst. Some of them might even be disappointed when Longarm arrested him—or shot him.

"We were about to stop for lunch," Guinevere went on. "Would you like to join us, Mr. Parker? I packed plenty of food in the basket."

Longarm pondered the invitation, but not for long. He nodded and said, "That sounds mighty nice. I'm much obliged, ma'am."

Archer might be mad as a hatter in his own way, but Guinevere seemed sane enough. And Longarm was in the habit of accepting most invitations he received from good-looking gals. Besides, from the sound of what Guinevere had said, they had been staying in Greenwood for a while, and he might be able to find out some more about Dog McCluskey's habits from them.

Archer retreated into the back of the wagon to tend to the butterfly he had captured. As Guinevere picked up the reins, Longarm asked, "Would you like for me to climb up there and handle that team for you, ma'am? I can tie my horse to the wagon and let him follow us."

"I assure you, Mr. Parker, that's not necessary," Guinevere replied with a smile. "I'm perfectly capable of handling these brutes. I've done a considerable amount of the driving since Roy and I came out here."

She flapped the reins and called out to the horses in a surprisingly strong voice, and the animals got moving. As the wagon rolled across the plains, Longarm turned his horse and fell in alongside it so he could continue talking to the young woman.

"Are you a butterfly collector, too?" he asked.

"Goodness, no. I sometimes help Roy with his collection, and I admire their delicate beauty, but I wouldn't say that I'm a collector." She lowered her voice before she went on, although it was unlikely that Archer would hear her, shut up in the back of the wagon like he was. "You see, Roy can be rather . . . absentminded. He gets so interested in what he's doing that he might forget to eat and sleep if someone didn't remind him. That's one of the drawbacks to being a genius, I suppose."

"Smart fella, is he?"

"Oh, yes. He's a member of the Philadelphia Academy of Science and Exploration and has mastered numerous scientific disciplines."

Longarm nodded. He had an idea that Roy Archer was probably pretty well-to-do, most likely from family money, and used that wealth to pursue those scientific interests Guinevere had mentioned. Longarm had encountered Eastern dudes like that on several occasions. Often, they ran into trouble when they came West, because they expected things on the frontier to be like they were back East. He'd had to pull their fat out of the fire more than once.

With all the tension between Carlton Barstow's Boxed B spread and the sodbusters who were moving into this valley, it might not be a good idea for the Archer siblings to be wandering around out here. They might stumble into a dangerous ruckus. But Longarm suspected that Roy Archer would scoff at the idea if he tried to warn him. Archer wouldn't want anything to interfere with his butterfly chasing.

They came to a small creek, and Guinevere brought the wagon to a halt on the grassy bank. No trees grew here to provide shade, but as Archer emerged from the back of the vehicle, he unfastened a couple of catches on one side of it and raised a panel on hinges to form an awning that he propped up with poles that folded down from it.

Longarm had watched the procedure as he was dismounting, and now he said, "That's a pretty smart setup. You carry your shade around with you."

"You like it?" Archer asked. Longarm could tell he was pleased by the praise. "I designed it myself, you know."

"Roy is very ingenious," Guinevere said as she reached into the back of the wagon and brought out a small folding table and a couple of stools. She set them up underneath the awning.

"All the comforts of home," Longarm commented.

"Yes, indeed. There's even enough room inside the wagon so that we can sleep in it if we have to."

Guinevere lifted a large picnic basket from inside the wagon. Longarm offered to help her with it, but she refused.

"You're our guest," she said. "In fact, you can have my chair—"

"Wouldn't hear of it," Longarm broke in. "You just sit right down, ma'am. I've hunkered by so many campfires that not having a place to sit don't bother me a bit."

Guinevere opened the basket. "While I'm getting the food ready, why don't you show Mr. Parker the specimens you've collected, Roy?"

Archer's face lit up with excitement. "What an excellent idea! Come along, Mr. Parker."

To be honest, Longarm would have preferred staying outside the wagon so that he could talk to Guinevere and watch her easy, graceful movements as she took food from the basket and placed it on the table. But he didn't want to be rude to Archer, so he said, "Sure," and climbed into the wagon after the lepidopterist.

A worktable had been built into the wagon along one wall, and above it several display boards were hung on hooks. A dozen different types of butterflies of all sizes and colors, most of them brilliant, were spread out and fastened to those boards by small pins that had been inserted through their wings. It looked sort of cruel to Longarm, but he knew the butterflies had been dead before they were pinned up there. Still, he thought the little critters were prettier when they were alive and flying around, rather than dead and stuck to a board. He wasn't interested in studying them, though, so he supposed that might make a difference.

Archer began rattling off the scientific and common names of the various types of butterflies. Longarm nodded, but he wasn't really paying much attention. Most of Archer's words went in one ear and out the other. Longarm was glad when Guinevere called them from outside the wagon to come and eat.

They climbed out of the vehicle and went under the awning. Guinevere had laid out a small but tasty feast on the table, including fried chicken, roasted ears of corn, and biscuits. Longarm enjoyed the meal. As he ate, he asked, "What sort of place is Greenwood?"

"Just a typical Western community, I suppose," Archer said. "We haven't visited all that many of them, so I suppose we're not the best judges of such things, are we, Guinevere?"

"It's not nearly as sophisticated as Philadelphia," she said. "Why, they don't even have an opera house."

"They have saloons, though," Archer said with a chuckle. "Plenty of them, in fact. And dance halls and gambling dens, too. Of course, I don't frequent such places, but it's difficult to overlook them. There's only the one hotel—"

"And it's not too bad," Guinevere put in, "although it could be a bit cleaner."

"And several restaurants and . . . What did that man call them the other day? Hash houses?"

Guinevere nodded. "That was it."

Longarm asked, "Any law there?"

"A constable, I believe. Or perhaps they call him a marshal. I'm not sure about that. But he has an office with a small jail attached."

"I'm surprised he hasn't tried to arrest Dog McCluskey. The Dog's a wanted man in a lot of different places."

"To tell you the truth," Archer said, "I wouldn't be surprised if Marshal Reeder is a bit frightened of Mr. McCluskey. I heard him say that as long as Mr. McCluskey doesn't break any laws in Greenwood, he intends to leave him alone. If you ask me, though, he just doesn't want any trouble with Mr. McCluskey."

That was probably about the size of it, Longarm mused. A small-town marshal usually didn't have to handle anything more troublesome than an occasional drunken cowboy. This fella Reeder probably figured that McCluskey would kill him if he tried to arrest him—and Reeder was likely right about that.

"Where does McCluskey spend most of his time?"

"At a saloon called the Double Diamond, I believe. I've seen him going in and out of there on several occasions."

Longarm nodded. He had figured he would find the Dog some place where whiskey and women were available.

Archer frowned. "You're awfully interested in Mr. McCluskey's whereabouts, Mr. Parker," he commented. "If I didn't know better, I'd say that you might be some sort of law-enforcement official. In fact, I *don't* know better. Are you a lawman?"

Guinevere had told him that her brother was smart, and Archer had just demonstrated that. Longarm didn't have any trouble telling bald-faced lies when it was necessary, so he laughed and said, "Me, a star packer? Not hardly. I just thought I might try to catch a glimpse of McCluskey myself, since he's such a famous desperado and all."

Archer nodded, seeming to accept Longarm's answer. "Well, you just go down to the Double Diamond when you get to town. You'll probably find him in there, having drinks bought for him by the hangers-on."

A moment later a butterfly flew past, and for a second Archer looked like he wanted to jump up and go after it.

Then he sighed and explained that he already had a specimen like that.

"The space I have for my collection is limited, you know," he said. "I can keep only the very best specimens."

Guinevere started talking about Philadelphia, asking Longarm if he had ever been there. He told her he hadn't. She sang the praises of the City of Brotherly Love for a while, as they finished their lunch, and then she began packing everything up, once again refusing Longarm's offer of help.

He had enjoyed meeting the two of them, especially Guinevere, but he still had a job to do, he reminded himself. He said, "I reckon I'll be riding on. It was mighty nice making the acquaintance of you folks. Maybe we'll run into each other again."

"I'm sure we'll see you in town," Guinevere said. She looked like she wanted to say something else, but she didn't.

Archer just bid good-bye to Longarm in a distracted manner and then went back into the wagon to play with his butterflies some more. Longarm waved at Guinevere and rode east, heading for Greenwood.

He hadn't gone very far when he came to another of the homesteads. Because he had eaten with the Archers, he didn't have any need to stop here after all, but since the trail took him close to the sod shanty, he decided he might as well stop and say howdy and maybe water his horse. Having a visitor would break the monotony for the folks who were trying to make a living off this land.

He was about fifty yards away from the soddy when an old man stepped out the door, pointed a rifle at him, and fired.

Chapter 6

The rifle bullet didn't come anywhere near Longarm, but just being shot at was enough to make him mad. He reined in and called, "Hey, take it easy, old-timer! What the hell's the idea?"

"The idea is you don't come any closer, mister," the old man said. "Try it and the next shot I fire won't be a warnin'! It'll go smack-dab in that ugly head o' yours!"

Now he was being downright insulting as well as hostile. Longarm reined in his temper and said, "You got me mixed up with somebody else, Pap. I don't mean you any harm."

The old-timer lowered the rifle a little and stared at Longarm in surprise. "How'd you know I was called Pap?"

Longarm gave him an honest answer. "Lucky guess. You look like a Pap."

"You ain't one o' Barstow's men?"

"Carlton Barstow of the Boxed B? I've heard of the man but never met him."

"Well, blazes, why didn't you say so?"

"You didn't give me a chance to before you tried to part my hair with hot lead!"

The old man lowered the rifle the rest of the way, and

damned if he didn't chuckle. "If I'd wanted to part your hair, son, I'd've done it. Where I growed up, back in the Tennessee hills, a boy who couldn't shoot the eyes out of a squirrel at a hundred paces was a mighty poor shot."

"Well, where I grew up in West-by-God Virginia, we shot their eyes out at *two* hundred paces." Longarm wasn't sure why he felt compelled to trade brags with this crotchety old pelican, but he did.

"Is that so?" Pap tugged on his white beard. "Well, I didn't even have to shoot 'em. When them squirrels saw me comin', they just give up and fell dead out of the trees, 'cause they knew I was gonna get 'em anyway."

Longarm grunted in disdain. "That whopper was old when Davy Crockett spun it about coons."

Pap glared at him for a moment longer, then said, "You sure you ain't a Barstow man?"

"I'm positive."

"Or a Hell Rider?"

Longarm frowned. "I don't know what a Hell Rider is, but I'm pretty sure I ain't one."

The old man waved a scrawny arm. "Well, then, ride on in. Ain't nobody gonna say that Pap Reynolds ain't hospitable."

Longarm rode up to the soddy and dismounted, ground-hitching the horse. He looked around and saw that there was a well and a small vegetable garden beside the shack, and the acreage behind it had been plowed and planted. He couldn't imagine a much harder way to make a living than hardscrabble farming. He'd take being shot at by desperadoes over trudging along behind a plow, any day of the week.

"Custis Parker," he introduced himself.

Pap shook hands with him. The old-timer's hand was gnarled and work-roughened. "You're a big 'un, ain't you?" he said as he looked up at Longarm. "Sorry I called you ugly. You ain't, really. Look sort of like an Injun, though."

Years of exposure to sun and wind had cured Long-arm's hide to the color of old saddle leather, and he knew his high-cheekboned face had a certain Indian cast to it. He didn't take offense at Pap's comment, having known plenty of red men who were fine folks, even though they weren't all noble savages like some folks back East wanted to believe. Mr. Lo, like any other man, could be good or bad or anywhere in between.

"Help yourself to water," Pap said with a gesture toward the well. "Your hoss, too."

Longarm went over and drew a bucket, then used the dipper that was hanging from a nail on the framework over the well to get himself a drink before he set the bucket on the ground for the horse. He looked at Pap and said, "Been having trouble with this fella Barstow, have you?"

It was still none of his business, but he figured since he had heard some of the story from the Boxed B riders he'd encountered, he might as well take a listen to the other side from one of the sodbusters.

"Aw, Barstow's a dang land hog. Figures since this was all open range when he first come out here, it ought to stay that way from now on. He acts like he owns everything west o' Greenwood, when the truth is he ain't got no right to any but just part o' the range. The rest of it was all gov-'ment land, and me and some others staked claims on it and been provin' up ever since."

"Barstow doesn't care about that, though?"

"I should hope to smile he don't! Says we got no right to be here and he'll see us all gone or dead, whichever way we want it."

"What about the law?" Longarm asked. "It has to be on your side."

Pap snorted in disgust. "County seat is so far east o' here we don't see the sheriff 'cept once in a blue moon when he comes around to drum up votes for the next election. He don't care what happens over here. The nearest law is the marshal in Greenwood, and he's just the town badge toter. Reeder ain't too diligent about enforcin' even that much law, neither."

That matched up with what Roy and Guinevere Archer had said about the local star packer. Longarm figured he couldn't look to Marshal Reeder for any help when it came time to arrest Dog McCluskey. That was all right. Longarm was used to playing a lone hand.

It occurred to him that Pap hadn't asked him to come inside, out of the sun. That was a little unusual. Most Westerners would extend such an offer to a visitor.

Maybe the old-timer had womenfolks in there and didn't want Longarm to see them. Some men were cautious about letting strangers know that any females were around. Most of the time a decent woman would be safe with even the roughest hard case, but there were occasional lobos who didn't care about anything except getting what they wanted.

Something else occurred to Longarm, and he asked, "What are those Hell Riders you mentioned?"

Pap spat, shuffled his feet, and looked embarrassed. "Aw, just forget about that. Don't want you thinkin' I'm crazy as a loon."

"I wouldn't think that," Longarm assured him. His curiosity was up now. "You can go ahead and tell me."

"Well . . ." Pap tugged at his beard again. "For the past month or so, some strange things have been goin' on around here at night. Crops have been trampled, livestock shot, wells caved in, and other mischief like that. A few of the fellas have got themselves shot tryin' to fight back."

"Sounds like things cowboys would do to try to run off homesteaders."

"Yeah, most of us sorta figure that Barstow's behind it, since he's been so outspoken about gettin' rid of us. What makes it all so strange is that the varmints who've been raidin' the farms . . . well, their heads are on fire."

Longarm just looked at the old man.

Pap returned the stare for a few seconds, then snatched the battered old hat off his nearly bald dome and slammed it to the ground. He started jumping up and down on it and yelled, "I knowed it! I knowed I shouldn't say nothin'! You think I'm teched in the head!"

Longarm reached out to grab the old-timer's arm. "Settle down, Pap, settle down!" he said. "I don't think you're crazy."

"You don't?" Pap looked like he didn't believe it. "Then maybe you're the one who's crazy."

"When a man tells me he's seen something with his own eyes, I tend to believe him," Longarm said. "Have you seen these so-called Hell Riders or just heard about them?"

Pap picked up his hat and started brushing it off. The headgear was already in such bad shape that being thrown on the ground and jumped on didn't appear to have hurt it.

"I seen 'em myself," he said without looking up. "Last night, in fact. They raided the place, came in a-shootin' and a-howlin'. I'd heard other folks talk about them, but that was the first time I'd seen 'em with my own eyes, like you said." A shudder went through him. "Spookiest thing you ever seen. They look like men, except where their heads ought to be is just a bunch o' flames."

Longarm let that bizarre statement pass for the time being, unsure what to make of it. "What happened?" he asked.

"Me an' Claire forted up inside the soddy and fought 'em off. A shack made o' dirt won't burn, and the walls are thick enough to stop a bullet, so as long as a fella's got plenty o' food, water, and ammunition, he can hold off an army in a place like this."

Longarm nodded in understanding, having defended more than one soddy in his eventful life. "Who's this Claire you mentioned?"

"Mighty inquisitive gent, ain't you?"

"No offense. You were the one who brought up the name."

"Claire's my granddaughter," Pap said. "It's just me an' her. We ain't got no other kinfolks left, neither of us."

Longarm inclined his head toward the soddy. "She inside?"

"Nope. Gone to town for supplies."

"You let a girl ride around by herself?" Longarm asked with a frown.

Pap chuckled. "Them Hell Riders don't come around in the daylight, and anybody else who was foolish enough to tangle with Claire would soon regret it. Gal's pricklier than I am, and a better shot with a handgun."

"I'll keep my eyes out for her, then. Taking potshots at me might run in the family."

"Don't bother her and she won't bother you," Pap told him. "You headed for Greenwood?"

"Yep." Longarm didn't mention what he intended to do once he got there.

"You'll probably run into her between here and there, then."

"You get into town very much yourself?"

Pap shook his head. "Naw, I stay pretty close to home. Never have cared much for settlements. Don't like bein' crowded. But it's good for a gal to get out and be around other folks sometimes. That's why I let Claire go in and pick up our supplies. Young gal like that don't need to just be around an ol' prairie lizard like me all the time."

Longarm's horse had finished drinking. There was no reason for the big lawman to linger here any longer. A time or two he thought he had noticed Pap casting a nervous glance toward the open door of the soddy, as if there were something in there he didn't want Longarm to see, but although that made Longarm curious, he didn't think it justified him forcing his way in for a look-see. And since the old-timer didn't get into Greenwood very often, chances were he didn't know anything about Dog McCluskey.

He said, "Well, it was nice meeting you, Pap," and reached for the horse's reins. "Maybe I'll stop in again sometime . . . if you promise not to take a shot at me."

"Can't promise that. I'm old, and I'll have likely forgot who you are by then."

Longarm laughed and swung up into the saddle. He lifted a hand in farewell and rode east toward Greenwood.

He hadn't gone very far when he noticed a cloud of dust rising in the air ahead of him. That much dust meant that several riders were on the move, and they were coming fast toward him. He reined in and waited to see what was going to happen.

He didn't have to wait for very long. A lone rider appeared in the distance, galloping hard. A moment later several more men on horseback came into sight, and it was obvious they were chasing the first hombre.

Longarm frowned. Either that lone rider had done something wrong, in which case he needed to be stopped, or he was in the right and was being ganged up on, and Longarm didn't like that. Whichever was true, it looked like he was going to have to take cards in this game.

A moment later, that possibility became a certainty. The rider being pursued came close enough for Longarm to see long brown hair streaming in the wind.

That "hombre" was a woman.

Chapter 7

When the stranger was gone, Pap came back into the soddy and looked at Matt O'Hara, who sat propped up in the rope bunk against one wall, a pistol clutched in his hand.

"All right, I played along with what you wanted, mister," Pap said in a hard voice. "Now you're gonna have to tell me what the sam hill this is all about."

"That fella rode on?" Matt asked, his voice husky with strain. He thought he had heard the hoofbeats as the horse left, but he wanted to be sure.

"Yeah, he's gone."

"Was he . . . a lawman?"

Pap stared at him for a long moment. The old man's eyes narrowed with anger. "I knowed it!" he burst out at last. "I knowed it! You're nothin' but a low-down owlhoot, runnin' from the law."

"No!" Matt gave a vehement shake of his head, even though the motion made him dizzy. "No, that's not true, Pap."

"Then why was you a-feared that hombre was a badge toter?"

Matt sighed. "There was a posse chasing me yesterday, but I'm not an outlaw. I swear it."

"Why was a posse after you?"

"Well . . . I sort of . . . tried to rob a bank. But there was some trouble, and the teller got shot—"

Pap swung the barrel of his rifle up. "I knowed it," he said again. "Not only a bank robber, but a dadblasted killer, too! Gimme that gun."

Matt had no choice. He reversed the pistol and extended it butt-first toward the old man. Pap edged closer, keeping the rifle pointed at Matt with one hand while he used the other to snatch the revolver out of the younger man's grip. He backed away holding both weapons.

"It didn't happen the way you think," Matt said. "I didn't go in there intending to hurt anybody."

"But you went in intendin' to hold up the place, right?"

"I had to. I was going to lose my ranch if I didn't put my hands on two thousand dollars!"

Pap's lip curled. "I ain't interested in your excuses, boy. A thief is a thief is a thief, and so's a killer."

"I don't *know* that Harvey's dead. And I didn't mean to shoot him at all."

"You ever heard what the road to hell's paved with?"

Matt sighed. "I ought to. Seems like I've been on it long enough."

"I wish that fella Parker *had* been a lawman. If he was, and if I'd knowed then what I know now, I'd've sure turned you over to him, 'stead of agreein' to keep quiet about you bein' here."

Matt had been stronger when he woke up that morning, although his side still hurt where the bullet had knocked a chunk out of it, and his head swam whenever he moved too fast. But when Claire had changed the bandages and checked the wound, she had nodded in satisfaction and said, "Looks like it'll heal up without too much trouble, as long as you take it easy."

He'd been right—with the powder-smoke smudges scrubbed off her face, she was mighty pretty. The man's shirt and trousers she wore were sort of baggy on her, but every so often as she moved around, he got an idea of how nicely built she was, with a young, firm, slender body under those clothes. He was careful not to let her catch him looking at her like that, though, because he already knew she was both sharp-eyed and sharp-tongued.

Pap had gone out as soon as it was light to see if he could find the man Matt had shot the night before. "I want to see what one o' them varmints looks like after his burnin' head's done gone out," the old-timer said.

But when he came back to the soddy a little later, he reported that there was no sign of the Hell Rider.

"Either he wasn't dead, or the rest o' them hellions carried his body off. Don't really matter, he's gone either way." Pap had held out his hand. A six-gun lay on the callused palm. "Found this layin' outside, though. Reckon you must've dropped it when Claire shot your hoss out from under you last night."

"Well, I thought he was one of them," she said.

Matt had reached for the gun, prompting Claire to continue, "Wait a minute, Pap. I'm not sure it's a good idea for you to give that Colt back to him."

"It's his gun."

"Yeah, but I don't want him using it on us."

Matt had sighed at that comment. "You folks saved my life. I didn't mean you any harm to start with, like I told you before, and I sure don't now."

Claire had squinted at him for a long moment before nodding. "All right, but we'll be keeping a mighty close eye on you, Mr. O'Hara."

"Call me Matt," he had said for some reason.

"I'll call you Mr. O'Hara, thank you very much."

Not long after that, Claire had announced that she was riding to the nearby settlement of Greenwood to buy some supplies. She and Pap were running low on sugar and salt and a few other goods.

"There's a settlement close by here?" Matt had wanted to know.

"'Bout a mile and a half east o' here," Pap had explained.

That was news to Matt. In his mad flight the day before, he must have galloped by the town without ever noticing its lights, because he had come from the east and should have passed it. That was how shaken he had been by everything that had happened.

Claire had seemed a little reluctant to leave her grandfather there alone to watch Matt, but in the end she had saddled up the one horse they owned and ridden off toward Greenwood.

Matt sat up on the bunk with a pillow propped behind him and sipped at a cup of coffee. Pap had spent the morning tending to chores around the place, including using his mules to drag off the body of the dead horse, which had no brand other than an unreadable "skillet of snakes" common in Mexico and along the border. He put the body in a nearby gully and caved in the bank on it. Then he had come inside and fixed a simple meal of cold salt pork and biscuits left over from breakfast. The two men talked as they ate. Matt could tell that Pap was curious about him, so he steered the conversation around to other subjects.

That wasn't very hard to do. All he'd had to say was, "What in blazes are those Hell Riders, anyway?"

"Some say they're just men. That's what Claire believes. But you seen 'em for yourself, Matt, and I don't know about you, but I never seen no man who could live through havin' his head turned into a blazin' torch like that."

"No, I never did, either," Matt had agreed.

"But whether they's men or monsters, there ain't much doubt that they're workin' for Carlton Barstow. None o' the cattlemen around here care overmuch for us homesteaders, but I reckon they'd all tolerate us if it wasn't for Barstow. He's got a powerful hate for anybody who tills the soil."

"Why does he feel like that?"

Pap had given a rueful shake of his head. "I don't know, unless he's one o' those fellas who's just got to get his way all the time. Some folks are born like that, full o' anger and convinced can't nobody ever be right but them."

Remembering Josiah Phelps, Matt had nodded in agreement. That was a pretty good description of the banker from his hometown. In a way, Matt was mighty glad he hadn't wound up with Phelps as his father-in-law. He would have had to put up with the man's sneers and superior attitude for the rest of his life.

"Anyway, Barstow's made it plain as the nose on his face that he's gonna force out all the homesteaders. That's why everybody thinks he set them night riders on us. Sure would like to know how they manage to set their heads on fire, though," the old-timer added.

It was while the two of them were talking that they had heard a horse approaching. "Looks like a stranger," Pap had announced from the doorway when he took a look. "Big hombre. Ain't never seen him before."

Cold fear slid along Matt's veins. Chad Haimes was a good-sized gent. Maybe the posse had turned back but the marshal was continuing the search on his own. In a strained voice, Matt had asked, "You think you could keep him outside, Pap, and not let him know I'm in here?"

That brought a suspicious squint from the old man.

"Please," Matt said. "I'll explain everything later."

Pap hesitated. Matt thought about threatening him with the pistol, but that wouldn't do any good, he realized. That would just convince Pap not to trust him.

"All right. But when he's gone, you're gonna have to tell me what this is all about."

Now everything had come out, and Pap knew the truth about him. Matt hated what he saw in the old man's eyes. Pap looked at him like he was as disgusting as a bug squashed on the sole of a boot.

"Claire was right," Pap went on. "I never should've given your gun back to you. Reckon we're lucky you didn't murder us both."

"I wouldn't hurt you," Matt declared. "Like I said, you saved my life."

Pap snorted. "Things like that don't mean much to an owlhoot."

Matt looked down at the floor and asked, "What are you going to do?"

"I ain't decided yet. When Claire gets back from town, I've got a good mind to tell her to turn around and ride right back there to fetch the marshal. Fella like you oughta be locked up where he can't hurt nobody else." Pap shrugged. "I'd do it, too, but I'm a-feared Reeder wouldn't come back with her. He'd tell her that a bank robbery and murder somewheres else ain't any o' his business."

Matt wished Pap would stop referring to what he had done as murder. For one thing, he didn't know for sure that Harvey Lapreste was dead, and for another he hadn't meant to shoot the teller.

"Ain't no other law close by," Pap went on. "I'll talk it over with Claire and see what she wants to do, but we may have to just tell you to move on. The law'll catch up to you sooner or later. Luck always plays out for your kind."

Matt didn't know about that "your kind" business, but luck did appear to have played out on him, all right. "Did you find my horse?" he asked in a dull voice.

"Didn't see hide nor hair of it."

"Are you going to give me back my gun?"

Pap's derisive snort was all the answer Matt needed to that question.

"So, you're going to turn me out, on foot and unarmed, with a bullet hole in my side?"

"That slug just grazed you. You'll be all right . . . least-ways until you wind up behind bars or at the end of a hang rope."

"I can't believe you'd do that," Matt said. "I tried to help you. I shot one of those Hell Riders."

"And we're obliged to you for that, if it really happened. I ain't seen no proof of it."

Anger welled up inside Matt. Now the old man thought he was lying about what had happened the night before.

"Don't you even want to know why I did what I had to do?"

"You didn't *have* to turn crooked. Nobody does."

"The banker in the town close to my ranch called in my loan," Matt went on, determined now to make the old man listen whether Pap wanted to or not. "He didn't have any reason to do it. I'd been making my payments just like I was supposed to. But he called in the whole amount when his daughter decided she didn't want to marry me after all."

"Sounds like the gal must've found out what sort of hombre you really are."

"I never did a damned thing wrong in my life!" Matt burst out. "Nothing dishonest, anyway. I just worked hard and tried to make my spread amount to something. Just like you try to make this farm successful. Are you beholden to anybody, Pap?"

The old-timer scowled at him. "Just the fella who owns the general store in town. I owe him a mite."

"What if you owed him two thousand dollars, and he said you had to pay it right away or you'd lose this place? What would you do then?"

"I don't know, but I sure as shootin' wouldn't go try to rob a bank!"

Matt leaned back against the pillow behind him and sighed. "Don't be too sure about that. Until you've looked that sort of trouble in the eye, don't be too sure."

Pap glared but didn't say anything. After a minute, Matt resumed, "I didn't mean to hurt anybody. I wouldn't have even fired a shot if the marshal hadn't come into the bank at just the wrong time and started shooting at me. The

63

teller reached across the counter and grabbed my gun. It went off. That's about all I can say. I lit a shuck out of there and wound up here."

Matt searched for the slightest bit of sympathy in the old-timer's gaze but didn't see any in Pap's steely eyes. Well, he had tried to make Pap understand, he told himself. That was all he could do.

"If you want me to leave," he said, "I will."

"Wait'll Claire gets back," Pap said. "That gal's smart as a whip. I ain't makin' up my mind about nothin' until I've had a chance to talk to her."

Matt nodded. At this point, he was glad for any small reprieve he could get. The longer it was before he was forced to leave, the more he could rest and get some of his strength back.

The sudden drumming of hoofbeats made Pap's head jerk up. Matt heard them, too, and said, "Maybe that's her now." His respite hadn't lasted long.

Pap shook his head. "No, that ain't her, not unless she's got somebody with her. They's several hosses comin' this way."

He picked up his rifle and went to the door. Matt's gun was tucked behind the old piece of rope that was tied around Pap's skinny waist to serve as a belt. Pap swung the door open to look out, and Matt saw the old man stiffen.

"It's that blasted Carlton Barstow," Pap said, "and he's got some o' his gun-wolves with him."

Chapter 8

Longarm pulled his Winchester from the saddle boot and waited as the pursuit approached him. As the rider in front came closer, he was able to see not only the long brown hair blowing out behind her head, but also the way the wind pressed her shirt against her body so that it hugged the good-sized mounds of her breasts. No mistaking now the fact that she was female.

She had been throwing frantic glances over her shoulder at the men chasing her, but as she looked forward again she seemed to spot Longarm for the first time. She must have thought that he was one of her enemies who had somehow gotten in front of her, because she jerked hard on the reins and tried to veer her mount away from him. She was too rough with the bit, though, and tried to make the horse take the turn too fast. The animal reared, stumbled, and went down in a welter of billowing dust and flailing hooves.

Grim-faced, knowing that the girl could have been hurt in the fall, Longarm galloped over to her and swung down out of the saddle almost before his horse had come to a stop. There wasn't much wind and the cloud of dust was slow to clear. The fallen horse kicked a few times and then managed to get up, moving away with skittish, prancing steps. Longarm tried to wave some of the dust aside as he stalked toward the spot where the woman had taken her tumble.

He heard a dust-choked cough, then the metallic ratcheting of a six-gun being cocked. "D-Don't come a step closer, mister!" she threatened. "I'll b-blow your damn head off if you do!"

Longarm stopped in his tracks and waited for the rest of the dust to clear. When it did, he saw her sitting on the ground a few yards away, a revolver gripped in both hands as she pointed it at him. He said, "I mean you no harm, miss."

Hoofbeats thundered up nearby.

"But I ain't so sure about those fellas," Longarm added as he turned to face the riders who had been chasing the woman. That meant turning his back on the gun she was pointing at him, but he figured the other men were the real threats.

There were half a dozen of them. Hard-faced hombres in range clothes. They hadn't been shooting at the girl, but they could have if they wanted to, because they were all gun-hung and carried repeaters in saddle sheaths. Longarm didn't like the looks of them, he thought as they reined in.

The feeling seemed to be mutual. The hard cases all glared at him, and one of them demanded, "Who the hell are you?"

Longarm was actually glad the man had asked the question, because that should convince the girl he wasn't one of them and lessen the odds of her shooting him in the back. With the Winchester held at a slant across his chest, he said, "I could ask the same thing of you, old son."

"You could," the hombre said with a sneer, "but there's six of us and one o' you, so I reckon you'd better answer first."

Longarm gave him a tight smile and hefted the Winchester a little. "The fifteen rounds in this repeater outvote you."

66

That drew even darker scowls. "You can't get all of us, damn you!" the spokesman said.

"Probably not, but I figure at least half of you will die before I go down. How do you boys feel about two-to-one odds on dying?"

The spokesman leveled an arm and pointed at the girl. "That slut's a damn thief! Maybe you ought to know what the game is before you sit in, mister."

"That's a lie!" the girl shouted. "I never stole a thing in my life!"

Longarm noted in passing that she didn't deny being a slut, but he figured that was just an oversight. Or not. Didn't really matter at the moment.

After her protestation of innocence, a long, tense moment of silence passed. Finally, the man who seemed to be in charge of the riders said in disgust, "Ah, hell, it ain't worth getting shot over. Come on, boys." He started to turn his horse.

"Hold on there," Longarm said. "Don't you think you ought to apologize to the lady for chasing her and calling her names?"

He heard her scrambling to her feet behind him. "That's not really necessary," she said. "Just let them go."

"No, they need to learn some manners," Longarm insisted. His dander was up.

The hard cases stared at him in disbelief. "The odds are still six to one against you, you dumb bastard," the spokesman said. He was a stocky, heavy-jawed man with curly brown hair showing under his dusty, thumbed-back Stetson.

"Six to two," the girl said as she stepped up alongside Longarm. The revolver was still gripped in her hand. "And I'm a good shot, too, Abilene. Chances are more than three of you will die."

The man called Abilene glared at her with hate glittering in his piggish eyes. After another of those nerve-straining silences, he said between gritted teeth, "I reckon we're sorry for chasin' you. We didn't mean you no harm."

"What about the rest of it?" Longarm prodded.

Abilene sighed. "And I'm sorry for callin' you a thievin' slut."

The girl nodded and said, "All right. I guess that'll do."

Abilene jerked his head at his companions. "Let's get the hell out of here."

They turned their mounts and spurred the animals into a gallop, not being too careful about the amount of dust they stirred up in the process. Longarm squinted and thought about putting a round or two over their heads just to hurry them along, but he decided against it. Sheer guts and icy nerves had gotten him and the girl through this confrontation unscathed, and he didn't want to foul that up now.

The girl stood beside him with a look of intense dislike on her face and watched them ride off. She didn't holster her gun. Longarm kept the Winchester ready, too, just in case the men decided to double back and jump them.

Abilene and the other hard cases kept riding, though, until they disappeared in the distance to the east, toward the settlement of Greenwood. Only when they were gone did the girl let out her breath in a long sigh and slide her Colt back into the holster on her hip.

"I'm obliged for the help, mister," she said as she turned to Longarm. "Wouldn't have needed it, though, if it hadn't been for you."

Longarm frowned. "If that's true, then those hombres must've been a lot more harmless than they looked and acted."

"They never would have caught me if you hadn't spooked me and made my horse take that tumble."

"You sure about that? Looked to me like they were gaining on you a mite."

"My horse is faster than any of their nags. At least, he was. I hope he didn't hurt himself when he fell." She walked toward the still-skittish horse, talking to the animal in a soft, soothing voice as she approached.

"Hey!" Longarm called after her. "That's it? You're just going to ride off?"

She glanced back at him. "I said I was obliged. What the hell else do you want?" Her face reddened as she added, "Don't you believe that lying son of a gun Abilene. I'm no more a slut than I am a thief, so I'm not going off in the bushes with you just to say thanks for some help I wouldn't have needed in the first place if you'd tended to your own business and stayed out of mine."

Remembering what Pap Reynolds had said about his granddaughter being prickly, Longarm said, "Your name's Claire, ain't it?"

She stopped trying to catch her horse and looked at him. "How'd you know that?"

"I stopped at your grandfather's place a little while ago. He told me about you and said you'd gone to Greenwood for supplies. Said I might run into you on my way to town."

He didn't mention the other comments the old-timer had made.

"Yeah, that's my name," she admitted. "Claire Reynolds."

"I'm Custis Parker."

"I'd say I was pleased to meet you, Mr. Parker—that is, if I really was."

Longarm couldn't help but chuckle. Claire Reynolds was a nice-looking young woman, despite being full of piss and vinegar. Her face was covered with dust and dirt from the fall she had taken, and he found himself wanting to brush it off so he could get a better idea of how pretty she might really be. Instead, he kept his distance and slid his Winchester back in the saddle boot while she caught the reins of her mount.

"Just so I'll know what I'm getting into," he said, "do those varmints who were chasing you hang out in Greenwood?"

"Yeah, mostly at a saloon called the Double Diamond."

Longarm knew the name from the earlier conversation with Roy and Guinevere Archer. The Double Diamond saloon was Dog McCluskey's current stomping ground. Chances were the hard case called Abilene and the other men knew the Dog.

"Are they likely to make trouble for me when I ride into town?"

"I don't know. Don't go there if you're scared. Greenwood's not that much. Just ride around it."

Longarm's eyes narrowed. He didn't like being accused of cowardice, but at the moment he was more interested in information than he was in defending himself.

"What do they do there? They didn't look like cowhands."

Claire appeared to be getting impatient to be on her way, but she answered his question instead of mounting up and riding on to her grandfather's farm. "Nobody really knows what they do," she said, "but I can make a pretty good guess. They're hired guns working for a high-handed son of a bitch named Barstow."

Longarm had already started to wonder about that very thing, so he wasn't surprised by Claire's answer.

"Your grandfather mentioned there'd been some trouble between Barstow and the homesteaders hereabouts. Told me about a bunch of hombres called Hell Riders, too." Longarm frowned in thought and tugged at his right earlobe, then raked a thumbnail along the line of his jaw. "You reckon Abilene and his pards could be part of that gang?"

"I don't know, but they've always got plenty of money. You figure it out if you want. But I don't see what business of yours it is, anyway."

"None at all, I suppose. Just curious."

"Well, if you stopped at the farm, you know Pap's waiting for me. I don't want to worry him." She put her foot in the stirrup and stepped up onto the horse, swinging her leg over and settling astride the saddle just like a man. Long-arm had already noticed that she was a good rider while she was being chased by the hard cases.

He mounted up, too, and suggested, "Maybe I ought to ride back there with you, in case Abilene and those other rannies circle around and come after you again."

"There's not much chance of that. Anyway, I'm not far from home."

Longarm was oddly reluctant to let her go on her way. "Why were they chasing you?"

Claire hesitated, then said, "Mr. Gafford, the fella who owns the general store in Greenwood, told me I had to pay him some on what Pap and I owe him. I had a dollar and I gave him that, but he said it wasn't enough." Her face started to turn red again. "Said if I'd go in the back of the store with him for a while, he'd give us longer to pay up."

Longarm's eyes narrowed in anger. Again, this was none of his business, but he thought he might have a little talk with Mr. Gafford while he was in Greenwood, if the opportunity arose.

"You didn't go with him, did you?"

Claire gave a defiant toss of her head. "What in blazes do you think?"

"I think the fella's lucky you didn't stick that hogleg up his nose for making such an impertinent suggestion in the first place," Longarm said.

"Yeah, well, I thought about it. But I was so mad I just ran out of there instead. I had this sack of supplies with me, and Mr. Gafford hadn't totaled up yet what I owed him for it, so he carried on like I was stealing it."

"And Abilene and those other fellas heard that and used it as an excuse to come after you, I reckon."

Claire nodded. "They probably would have taken me back to town and turned me over to the marshal if they'd caught me . . . after they had some fun first. That's the sort of low-down skunks they are."

71

Longarm figured she was probably right. The way things were shaping up, the folks in these parts had quite a bit of trouble on their plates. A ruthless, land-hungry cattle baron, a bunch of night riders with burning heads, gun-slicks on the prowl . . . a lawman would have his hands full cleaning things up around here.

Unfortunately, all he'd come to do was arrest Dog Mc-Cluskey.

"Well, you be careful," Longarm told her as he gave the brim of his Stetson a tug. "I guess I'll head on to town."

"You best have eyes in the back of your head, Mr. Parker. Abilene looks like a backshooter to me, and he'll have a grudge against you now."

"I'll keep that in mind." Truth was, he always watched his back pretty careful-like. He wouldn't have survived this long if he hadn't.

They went their separate ways then, Longarm riding east while Claire headed west. But he glanced over his shoulder a time or two at her dwindling figure, wondering if he would ever see her again.

Chapter 9

Stiff with tension, Matt sat on the bunk as the horses continued to approach outside the soddy. Pap glanced over his shoulder at the young man, then grimaced and tugged the pistol from behind the rope belt around his waist.

"Here," he said as he tossed the weapon to Matt. "I won't leave any man unarmed while Barstow and that bunch o' hydrophobic skunks are around, even a murderin' bank robber like you."

Matt caught the gun, plucking it out of the air, and nodded a grim thanks to the old-timer. He had no quarrel with Carlton Barstow, other than the gratitude he felt toward Pap and Claire for helping him and his natural tendency to stick up for the underdog. He already had enough trouble in his life and wouldn't go out of his way to borrow more. But if a ruckus started, Matt intended to back Pap's play, whatever it was. Even though Matt was weak, he thought he could make it to the doorway—and he knew for damn sure that he was strong enough to pull a trigger.

"Stay there," Pap told him. "I'll handle this, just like I did with that fella Parker."

Matt nodded. "Yell if you need help."

Pap looked at him like he'd be damned before he'd take

help from a murderin' thief, but then he returned the curt nod, opened the door the rest of the way, and stepped outside. A moment later the horses came to a stop.

"Reynolds," a man said in a deep voice like gravel sliding down a hillside. "I thought I told you to get off my range."

"And I *know* I told you this ain't your range, Barstow," Pap responded. "If you want to see my deed from the gov-'ment, I'll be glad to show it to you."

"I don't give a hoot in hell about some worthless piece of paper. What some jackass in Washington says don't mean a thing out here. This is my range, and has been for more'n twenty years."

The door was still open a crack. Through that gap, Matt could see Pap standing stiff and straight, the rifle in his hands. Stubborn defiance seemed to come off him in waves. He said, "You was here before me, that's true enough, but the Cheyenne and the Arapaho was here before you. You took the land from them. If you got a right to it now, didn't they have a right to it then?"

"You're right," Barstow said, his every word clear to Matt inside the soddy. "I *took* this range. I fought those damn redskins for it, and I fought the blizzards in the winter and the droughts in the summer and the sickness that took half my herd and both of my sons. I *earned* this range, Reynolds. And you say it's yours because the government *gave* it to you."

Pap didn't answer for a moment. Then he said, "I reckon what you say is true, but I didn't make the law, and the law says this homestead is mine if'n I prove up on it, and I have. Ain't nothin' you can do about that."

"A damn soddy and some scraggly-ass vegetable garden ain't improvements," Barstow challenged. "And without them, you won't have a damn thing to show you were ever here causin' a blight on the land."

Pap shifted the rifle in his hands. "You threatenin' me, Barstow?"

"I'm sayin' I'm tired of warnin' you, you blasted old buzzard, and there's no tellin' what might happen one of these nights."

Matt swung his legs out of the bunk, fearful that this confrontation was about to escalate into violence. He felt a twinge in his side as he stood up, but the bandages around his torso were so tight that the wound didn't hurt much. For a second after he got to his feet, his head spun, so he had to wait for that to pass. But when it did, he walked in a stiff-legged gait to the door and pushed it all the way open.

The squeak of hinges made Pap turn his head to look at the soddy. The sound drew the attention of the unwelcome visitors, too. Several of them edged their horses around so they could face him head-on. Here and there a hand shifted closer to the butt of a gun.

"Who the hell are you?" demanded a big man with a seamed, leathery face and thick white hair under a black Stetson. Judging by his position slightly in front of the other men, the expensive ivory-handled, nickel-plated Colt on his hip, and the fancy saddle studded with silver conchos, this was Carlton Barstow. A rich and powerful man, and everybody he came in contact with had damned well better know it.

"I'm a friend of Mr. Reynolds's," Matt said as he inclined his head toward Pap, who didn't look too pleased about him putting in an appearance. Matt had the six-gun in his hand, but he kept it down at his side—for now.

Barstow grunted. "Looks like you've already run into some trouble, son. You're askin' for more by sidin' with this squatter."

"Like I said, he's a friend of mine," Matt said, as if that explained everything. And truth be told, out here in the West it sort of did.

Pap moved a little so that he was standing closer to Matt. The old-timer might not like him or trust him, Matt thought, but at the moment Pap wanted to present a united front to Barstow.

"You were threatenin' me, if I recollect right," Pap said. "Talkin' like you was gonna send night riders after me. You're a little late, Barstow. Them Hell Riders o' yours showed up last night. We give 'em what-for and sent 'em packin'. Even ventilated one o' the sons o' bitches."

Pap didn't specify which of the defenders had shot the Hell Rider, Matt noticed. He didn't know if the old man was doing that to protect him or for some other reason. It didn't matter. Barstow would be mad enough about losing one of his hired guns, no matter who had pulled the trigger. Pap wasn't telling Barstow anything that the cattle baron didn't already know, either. By now Barstow must have received a report from his flame-headed minions and known that the raid was a failure.

Those thoughts went through Matt's head in the second or two it took Barstow to frown and say, "What the hell are you talkin' about, you addlepated old fool? I've told you—hell, I've told anybody who'll listen—I don't have anything to do with those so-called Hell Riders. I've never even seen the bastards, and to tell you the truth, I ain't sure they even exist. Sounds like something an old coot like you would make up."

"Yeah, boss," one of the tough-looking riders with Barstow spoke up. "He's crazy."

"Crazy, am I?" Pap said as his temper got the best of him and he started to swing his rifle up. "I'll show you who's crazy, you spavined galoot!"

All of Barstow's men reached for their guns. In that instant, Matt knew what was going to happen. He and Pap could try to make a fight of it, but if they did, the outcome would not be in doubt. They would both wind up shot to pieces.

And if that happened, Claire would be left to deal with Barstow by herself. Stubborn though she might be, in the end she wouldn't stand a chance.

"Hold your fire!" he shouted as he lunged toward Pap and grabbed the rifle barrel, forcing it back down. "Damn it, don't shoot!"

Barstow's riders had their guns drawn by now, but they held off on the triggers as Matt struggled to keep Pap from starting the ball.

"Let go o' me, you blasted varmint!" Pap howled. "I'm gonna ventilate their sorry hides—"

"You're going to get yourself killed, that's what you're going to do," Matt said. "Is that what you really want, Pap? You really want to leave Claire to face these hombres by herself?"

His mention of Claire's name seemed to get through to Pap's anger-maddened brain. The old-timer stopped struggling so much. Matt had moved in front of him, facing him, so that Matt's back was to Barstow and the other men. When Matt looked over his shoulder, he found himself staring down the barrel of the cattle baron's ivory-handled Colt.

"We all saw what happened," Barstow said in a flint-hard voice. "The old coot tried to shoot me. We'd be justified in fillin' both of you with lead, right here and now. The law wouldn't touch us."

Matt stood there taking shallow breaths, knowing that his life, and Pap's, hung in the balance here. All Barstow had to do was press the trigger. His men already had their guns in their hands, and they were so keyed up that the roar of a shot would set them off. As inevitable as a stampede on a stormy night, they would start shooting and wouldn't quit pulling their triggers until their guns were empty and Matt and Pap were lying on the ground, riddled with bullets.

Then Matt looked past the riders and saw something that made the ice crystals already forming in his veins freeze solid. Still, it was a card he had to play.

"If you kill us, Barstow," he said, "you'll have to kill her, too. How do you think your men will feel about murdering an innocent girl?"

He nodded toward a spot in the distance where a lone rider had reined to a halt and sat there watching the confrontation in front of the soddy. The wind blew the rider's long hair around her head. Even though Matt had seen Claire only a couple of times and had been in pretty bad shape on the first occasion, he had no trouble recognizing her.

"It's the old man's granddaughter, boss," one of Barstow's men said as they all turned to look in the direction Matt had indicated.

"Damn it, I know who it is," the cattle baron said.

"She's close enough to see that Pap and I aren't threatening you," Matt said. "If you gun us down, it'll be cold-blooded murder, and Claire will be a witness to it."

"If she's close enough to see what's goin' on, she's close enough for us to catch her," Barstow pointed out. "Ain't that right, boys?"

Halfhearted murmurs of agreement came from several of the men, but none of them sounded too enthusiastic about the idea. They might be rough as a cob, they might have even been willing to go along with their boss and fill Matt and Pap with lead, but getting rid of a woman . . . that was different. It took a special kind of snake-blooded varmint to do that, and Matt could see that none of these men wanted to sink that low.

Barstow must have realized that, too, because he muttered, "Hell," and jammed that flashy pistol back in its holster. Glaring at Matt and Pap, he said, "This ain't over. This is still my range, and you're still a good-for-nothing squatter, old man. Sooner or later I'll have my way, by God, and you'd be wise not to push me into seein' how far I'll go!"

With that he yanked his horse around and put the spurs to it. The animal leaped forward in a gallop and left the place in a cloud of dust. Barstow's men holstered their weapons and turned to follow at a more reasonable pace. Most of them kept their faces expressionless, but a few couldn't help but look relieved they hadn't had to kill anybody today, especially Claire.

Pap and Matt watched them go. Neither man relaxed until the riders were several hundred yards away and still moving. Then Pap turned to Matt and said, "Don't you ever get in my way again when I'm fixin' to shoot somebody, boy."

"You would have gotten us both killed," Matt said. "What would that accomplish? What would have happened to Claire?"

"Don't you even say her name. Barstow and his bunch wouldn't have even knowed she was there if you'd just kept your trap shut."

"I took a chance," Matt admitted. "But it kept Barstow from murdering us."

Pap shook his head and glared. "You just keep puttin' down more marks against yourself, son."

That was the way his life had turned out, all right, Matt thought, but he didn't see any point in saying it.

Claire was riding toward the soddy now, moving fast across the prairie. She had her rifle across the saddle in front of her and looked ready to use it. Matt hoped that if shooting had erupted while Barstow and his men were there, Claire would have done the sensible thing and turned her horse around to ride as fast as she could for Greenwood, where she would be safe.

But he had a feeling that's not the way it would have gone at all. If Barstow and his men had opened fire, chances were Claire would have charged in all hell-bent-for-leather, firing that Winchester as she came, and gotten herself killed.

As she rode up and reined in, she said, "That was Barstow, wasn't it?"

"Yeah," Pap said. "Him and his coyotes."

"What did he want?"

Pap shrugged. "The same ol' thing. He started in a-blusterin' and a-blowin' about how this was his range and I'd better get off it and how if I didn't he was gonna run me off. Just like an ol' bull snortin' and pawin' at the ground."

"Old bulls are dangerous," Claire said. She looked at Matt. "What are you doing out of bed?"

Matt began, "I thought I'd lend Pap a hand—"

"Don't talk to him," Pap cut in. "The truth come out whilst you was gone. He's an outlaw, Claire, just like you figured he might be."

Her brown-eyed gaze hardened into a cold stare. "Is that true?" she demanded. "You're a no-good owlhoot?"

He opened his mouth to try to explain, but then, just like that, he didn't care anymore. She wouldn't believe him, no matter what he said. She wouldn't even try to understand that he'd had reasons for everything he had done, reasons that seemed good to him even if they didn't to anybody else. She and Pap both had already made up their minds about him, and nothing he could say or do was ever going to change them.

"I'm obliged to you for your help," he said without answering her question, "but I reckon I'd best be moving on."

"Moving on how?" Claire wanted to know. "Your horse ran off, remember?"

"I've still got two good legs."

"And a bullet hole in your side you seem to have forgotten about, too."

Pap said, "Let him go if he wants to, Claire. He's got his gun. That's more'n he deserves."

Claire looked back and forth between the two men. "Land's sakes, what happened here while I was gone?"

"It's not important," Matt told her. "You didn't trust me to start with. You thought I was one of the Hell Riders. Maybe I am."

Claire looked at him for a long moment, then said, "No,

I saw the way you stepped between Pap and Barstow. I don't know what in blazes you *are*, but I'm pretty sure you're not a Hell Rider."

That was something, anyway, Matt told himself. More than he expected. Probably more than he deserved. He turned toward the soddy. "I'll gather my gear, what little there is of it, and go."

Neither Pap nor Claire said anything. Didn't tell him to stop. He fully intended to do what he had just said he would do.

He would have, too, if the strain of the past half hour or so hadn't caught up to him at that very moment and made him pass out cold, facedown in the dirt.

Chapter 10

Winchester in hand, Longarm slipped back from the crest of the little hill about three hundred yards from the Reynolds place. The rise was just tall enough to keep him and his horse from being seen. He had bellied down just below the crest and thrust the barrel of the rifle over it. For several tense minutes, he had watched the showdown in front of the soddy. His instincts told him that the big fella on horseback was Carlton Barstow.

Longarm had no idea who the hombre was that had come out of the soddy to stand with Pap against the rancher and his hired guns. But Longarm wasn't going to sit there and watch the two men be gunned down. He had drawn a bead on Barstow, and at the first shot, he planned to put lead in the high-handed son of a bitch.

It hadn't come to that, and Longarm was glad. For one thing, Claire would have gotten mixed up in it, and he didn't want that.

It was because of Claire that he was here. The possibility that Abilene and those other gunnies could have circled around and been waiting for her had nagged at Longarm until he gave up, turned around, and followed her toward the farm, keeping far enough back so that she wouldn't know he was there.

The way she had stopped short and sat there on her horse staring at the place had been enough to alert Longarm to the fact that something was wrong. He had veered off to the side, found himself a place where he could see what was going on, and settled down to watch what developed.

Now Barstow and the other men were gone, and Claire was riding up to the soddy. Longarm knew she would be all right now, so he slid his rifle back in the saddle boot and picked up the reins. He led the horse for about a hundred yards, taking care to avoid a scattering of prairie dog holes, until he reached a place where he could mount up without being seen from the farm.

As he rode away, he remembered the way Pap had acted while he was there getting a drink for himself and for his horse. The old-timer had cast several nervous glances toward the door of the soddy. Someone less observant than Longarm might not have even noticed, but Longarm made his living—and stayed alive—by keeping his eyes and ears open.

Longarm hadn't been able to tell anything about the second man at the farm except that he moved around in a rather stiff manner, as if he were old or maybe hurt. Come to think of it, instead of a white shirt, that could have been bandages wrapped around him, Longarm thought.

Curious or not, it didn't have anything to do with him. But if he came back this way, after dealing with the job that had brought him here, he might stop by and say hello to Pap and Claire and whoever their mysterious visitor was.

It was late afternoon by the time Longarm jogged his horse down the main street of Greenwood, Kansas. The settlement had never been an actual cattle town, like Abilene, Hays, and Dodge City, because the railroad hadn't come here. The route of the iron horse ran farther south. But Greenwood still owed its existence to cattle because it had sprung into being as a supply point for the numerous ranches in the area. Now, with farmers beginning to move in as well, Greenwood's future seemed to be assured. Sodbusters needed supplies, too, and in the long run there would be even more of them than there were cattlemen.

For the time being, Greenwood was a young, bustling community. Its business district stretched for a couple of blocks along both sides of the main street. In these largely treeless environs, lumber for construction had to be freighted in from somewhere else, so nearly all the buildings were a single story, although several false fronts were in evidence. The Double Diamond saloon was one of only two buildings that had an actual second floor. The other establishment that could make that claim was the Greenwood Hotel.

Two churches, one Baptist, one Catholic, stood at the far eastern end of the street. On the western edge of town, the part Longarm came to first, was a scattering of sod huts and tar-paper shacks and buildings made of hastily nailed together unpainted planks. A town like Greenwood that made much of its living from the cowboys who worked on the surrounding ranches would have a fairly high percentage of whores, gamblers, and assorted riffraff among its citizens. Longarm figured most of them lived in this part of the settlement, although they would do their work in the saloons. On the eastern side of town, closer to the churches, would be the homes of the more respectable citizens.

The sun was a garish red ball on the horizon when Longarm drew rein in front of the Double Diamond and swung down from the saddle. He looped the reins around a hitch rail and studied the saloon, which would have been one of the largest buildings in town even without its second story. The front of the Double Diamond took up half a block, with its entrance in the center flanked by large windows. It must have cost a pretty penny to haul that much glass out here from Wichita. The name of the place was written in fancy gold script on both windows.

As Longarm took the single step up onto the boardwalk in front of the saloon, the batwings were thrust open from inside and several men emerged. Longarm turned his head away so they wouldn't notice him, but not before he recognized the heavy-jawed countenance of one of the men. It belonged to the hombre called Abilene. His companions were some of the men who had been with him when he was chasing Claire Reynolds.

Except for one. Longarm had never seen that gent in person—but he had seen drawings of him on reward dodgers. He recognized the lantern jaw, the small but vicious eyes, the arrogant sneer on the thin-lipped mouth.

Dog McCluskey.

The Dog was a tall, rangy varmint in a cowhide vest and narrow-brimmed black hat. He and Abilene and the other men turned away from Longarm on the boardwalk. Talking and laughing among themselves, they left the Double Diamond and headed for some unknown destination. Longarm couldn't help but glance at McCluskey's ass as the outlaw strolled away, but he couldn't see any sign of the infamous tail that had gotten the Dog his nickname. Longarm wondered if he kept it strapped down or some such, then pushed that thought from his head. It was bad enough he had even looked.

He pushed through the batwings and went into the saloon, which was crowded despite the relatively early hour. There were still some open spots at the long bar, so Longarm stepped up to the hardwood and caught the eye of the bald, mustachioed, apron-wearing drink juggler on the other side.

"What'll it be?" the bartender asked.

"Beer," Longarm told him. What he really wanted was a shot of Maryland rye, but they might not have Tom Moore in a place like this, and anyway, Longarm figured he ought to keep his head as clear as possible. Somehow, he wasn't surprised to discover that the man he was after seemed to be pards with some fellas who already had a grudge against him.

For a heartbeat, there on the street, he had thought about challenging McCluskey and getting it over with. But while Longarm had never been afraid of facing superior odds, as long as they weren't too overwhelming, he was sure that Abilene and the other men would have joined in the fracas and he would have had to deal with five or six gunnies instead of just one. Not only that, but quite a few people had been on the street, and he didn't want to run the risk of some innocent bystander being cut down when the lead started to fly.

No, even though it was frustrating in a way, he knew he had done the right thing by postponing the showdown with the Dog. He would bide his time and take McCluskey when the chances were better of doing so without endangering anyone else.

The bartender had drawn a mug of beer and set it in front of Longarm. "Six bits," he said in a surly voice.

Longarm dropped coins on the bar to pay for the drink and picked it up. The beer was bitter and barely cool, but it cut the trail dust. He drank half of it down before he lowered the mug.

"My, you are a big one, aren't you?"

The admiring comment made him look over at the woman who had come up to the bar beside him. It was obvious at first glance that she worked here. The gaudy, low-cut, spangled dress was enough to tell Longarm that much. She was short and lushly built. The creamy mounds of her large breasts threatened to spill out of the daring dress, which was also short enough to reveal calves clad in silk stockings. The stockings had seen better days, but then, so had the woman.

Still, she wasn't bad-looking, with a heart-shaped face under a heavy layer of war paint. Thick blond curls were piled on top of her head and decorated with a small red feather. The feather matched her bow of a mouth, which was smiling up at Longarm.

He wasn't really interested, but when it came to whores he was too softhearted to tell her that. So he just gave her a pleasant nod and said, "Howdy, ma'am."

"How'd you like to have supper with me, cowboy?" she asked. "Then when we're done, we can go upstairs and . . . have some dessert."

"It's tempting," Longarm said, and in a way, it was. She looked like she would be a bouncy-bottomed handful between the sheets. Bedding her would be mighty enjoyable. And he wasn't doing anything at the moment anyway. He had already spotted Dog McCluskey and knew his quarry was in town, and he had decided to wait for a more opportune time to brace the outlaw. So why not, he asked himself. Why the hell not?

He was just about to tell the gal that her suggestion sounded mighty fine to him when he glanced past her, over the batwings, and saw a familiar wagon roll by in the street outside. It was the vehicle belonging to Roy and Guinevere Archer.

Acting on impulse, Longarm smiled and said, "Maybe another time, honey."

"Are you sure?"

Longarm drained the rest of his beer and thumped the empty mug on the bar. "I'm afraid so."

She gave him a disappointed pout and said, "You'll be sorry you passed this up, cowboy. But you come on back any time you want and give me a try. Ask for Molly."

"I'll do that," he promised as he started toward the entrance. Behind him, Molly had already moved on to the next man at the bar and was leaning against him with her impressive bosom rubbing all over his arm. Longarm smiled to himself. Soiled doves were a mighty resilient breed.

He pushed the batwings aside and stepped out onto the boardwalk, turning his head to look for the wagon he had seen go by. He spotted it down the street, pulling up in front of the Greenwood Hotel. Taking long strides, the big lawman started in that direction.

Roy Archer was at the rear of the wagon, standing at the open door and reaching inside the vehicle to take something out. Longarm didn't see Archer's sister. Guinevere must have already gone into the hotel.

As Longarm approached, crossing the street at an angle toward the hotel, Archer removed a wooden case of some sort from the wagon and stepped up onto the boardwalk with it, heading for the double front doors of the hotel. Before he got there, a couple of men walking along the boardwalk got in his way, and Archer didn't see them. Longarm winced as the inevitable collision took place, staggering Archer and the man he had run into.

Archer let out a startled cry as the impact jarred the case from his hands. It fell to the boardwalk with a crash, the lid springing open and the contents spilling out with a clatter. The man Archer had collided with ripped out an angry curse and gave the Easterner a shove. "Watch out where the hell you're goin'," he said.

Archer caught his balance against the railing that ran along the front of the boardwalk. "I beg your pardon," he said. "I was thinking about my work—I'm easily distracted, you know—and didn't see you."

The two men looked at each other and laughed. It was an ugly sound. Both of them wore range clothes, and the slight sway to their walk had told Longarm that they had been drinking. They hadn't guzzled enough rotgut to be harmless, though. Instead, they were just drunk enough to be dangerous.

The one Archer had run into stepped closer to him and prodded him in the chest with a hard finger. "If you can't think and walk at the same time, mister, you ain't got no business bein' out here. Why don't you just go back to wherever the hell it is you came from?"

Longarm saw Archer's back stiffening and knew the lepidopterist was getting mad, too. "I'll leave whenever I'm finished with the work that brought me here," Archer declared. "Until then, I've apologized, and I expect you to be gentlemen enough to accept it."

Archer's angry reaction was justified. Problem was, even though he was in the right and the collision had been an accident, a butterfly chaser tangling with a couple of liquored-up cowboys was a disaster waiting to happen. It wouldn't matter who was right and who was wrong once they got through beating the hell out of him.

The two cowhands hooted with derisive laughter. "Greenhorn, you got a lot to learn, and we're just the hombres to teach you."

Archer sniffed. "Somehow, I doubt that men such as yourselves could teach me anything . . . except, perhaps, how to be a boorish lout."

Longarm sighed and shook his head as he reached the boardwalk. Now trouble was probably unavoidable, and if he didn't pitch in and give Archer a hand, the Easterner was in for the thrashing of his life.

The two cowboys looked at each other. "Did he just insult us?" one asked the other.

"Damned if I don't think he did," the second man said. His hands clenched into fists. "Let's whip the prissy little son of a bitch."

Longarm was about to call out to them and tell them to hold it, when Roy Archer let out a yell and went pure-dee crazy again.

Chapter 11

This time Archer wasn't running across the prairie waving a net at some butterfly, but his actions were just as swift and unexpected as they had been earlier in the day when Longarm had first encountered him.

Archer stepped closer to the cowboys and snapped a fist out in a short but wicked punch that landed with a solid smash in the middle of the nearest man's face. The other cowboy let out a profane yell and swung a haymaker at Archer's head. The Easterner ducked so that the blow passed harmlessly over the top of his planter's hat.

Archer bored in on the second man, hooking a left and then a right into his belly. The punches doubled the cowboy over, which put him in perfect position for Archer's next move. Archer grabbed the man's shoulders and shoved down. At the same time, he brought his knee up and it met the cowboy's face with devastating force. The man crumpled to the boardwalk with blood gushing from his nose.

The first cowboy had recovered from the stinging jab to the face that Archer had given him. Howling with rage, the man lunged at Archer, his arms outstretched and widespread, ready to sweep the Easterner into a crushing bear hug.

Instead, Archer's hands clamped around the cowboy's right forearm. He pivoted to the left, stuck out his right hip, hauled hard on the cowboy's arm, and sent the man flying up and over him in as neat a wrestling throw as Longarm had seen. It reminded him of some of the things he had seen Jessie Starbuck's friend Ki do.

The cowboy let out a startled yelp as he found himself sailing through the air. The cry was cut off short as he crashed down onto the boardwalk on his back. The impact made dust rise from his clothes. He twitched a couple of times and then lay there motionless, stunned into insensibility by the force of his landing.

With both of the cowboys now down, all the fight knocked out of them, Archer stepped back, brushed his hands off, and removed his hat so that he could sleeve away the beads of sweat that had appeared on his forehead. As Longarm stepped up onto the boardwalk, Archer glanced at him, then his eyes widened in recognition.

"Mr. Parker! How good to see you again."

Longarm slid a cheroot from his shirt pocket and put it in his mouth, leaving it unlit for the moment. "That was a mighty impressive fracas, professor," he said around the cheroot. "I was pretty sure those two hombres were going to give you a licking."

Archer looked down at the cowboys and said, "Yes, well, I've had to deal with ruffians like them before. I was a rather sickly, studious lad growing up, and as such I attracted bullies. I had to learn to take care of myself."

Longarm smiled. "I'd say you did a good job of it."

The fight, short though it had been, had garnered attention from folks on the street. Several of them stood around gaping. One of them said to Archer, "Mister, those two fellas ride for Carlton Barstow. He ain't gonna be happy when he hears about what happened to 'em."

"I'm certain I don't care if Mr. Barstow is happy or not," Archer replied.

One of the hotel doors was thrown open, and Guinevere rushed out onto the boardwalk. "Roy!" she said as she hurried over to her brother. "Someone in the hotel said you'd gotten into a fight. Are you all right, dear?"

"I'm fine," Archer told her. Longarm couldn't help but hear the note of pride in his voice. "Please don't concern yourself, Guinevere."

Longarm fished a lucifer out of his pocket and snapped it into life with an iron-hard thumbnail. He held the flame to the tip of the cheroot and set fire to the gasper. As he shook the match out and flipped it into the street, he said, "Let me give you a hand picking up that stuff you dropped, Archer."

The Easterner stepped forward as Longarm bent over the wooden case. "That's all right, Mr. Parker," he said. "I can manage. Please don't trouble yourself."

"No trouble," Longarm said. He gathered up a handful of hollow metal rods that looked as if they might screw together. As he placed them back into the case, he smiled and said, "Looks like you could make a mighty long-handled butterfly net with these."

Archer chuckled. "Well, sometimes it's difficult to sneak up on the little fellows. You have to capture them at a distance, so to speak." He gathered up more of the rods, along with some sort of apparatus that had a crank on it, and replaced them in the case. When they had picked up everything, he moved to close the lid, but before he could do so, Longarm pointed to a row of metal flasks held in leather loops inside the case.

"That where you keep your who-hit-John?"

"What?" Archer looked confused for a second before his expression cleared. "Oh, you mean whiskey! No, I'm afraid I'm not much of a drinker. Those are chemicals I use in killing, mounting, and preserving my specimens." He lowered the lid and snapped the catches closed.

The case had a handle on top of it. Longarm reached

down to grasp it. "I'll carry this for you. Seems to be pretty heavy."

"I can handle it, I assure you." Archer took the case from him. "But I appreciate the offer."

"Mr. Parker," Guinevere spoke up. "You had lunch with us today. Would you care to share supper with us in the hotel dining room? Or have you eaten already?"

"As a matter of fact, I haven't," Longarm told her. "It's mighty nice of you to extend the invitation. I reckon I'll accept."

"I'll just take this on up to my room," Archer said, hefting the case. "Guin, why don't you and Mr. Parker go on to the dining room and secure a table for us? I'll be back down in a few moments."

"All right," she agreed. She offered her arm to Longarm. "Mr. Parker?"

He linked his arm with hers and walked with her through the hotel lobby toward the arched entrance leading into the dining room. Now that the fight was over, the small crowd had broken up in a hurry. Longarm glanced through the large window in the front of the hotel and saw the two cowboys picking themselves up from the boardwalk. They were both groggy, and the one whose nose had been pulped by Archer's knee had blood all over his face. They staggered away. Longarm hoped they would put this fracas behind them and not come back later, looking to settle the score with Archer.

He and Guinevere went on into the dining room and were seated at one of the tables. While they were waiting for the plump, white-aproned waitress to bring them coffee, Guinevere asked, "Did you witness the altercation between my brother and those cowboys, Mr. Parker?"

"Call me Custis, and yep, I sure did. Fact is, I was planning to step in and give him a hand, but he didn't need any help. He handled those two hombres without much trouble at all."

She smiled. "Yes, Roy has always been adept at pugilism. You wouldn't think so to look at him, would you?"

"No offense, but I sure wouldn't," Longarm agreed. "He seems like the sort of fella who'd be better with his brain than his fists."

"It helps to be good with both."

Longarm nodded. He had found that to be true in his line of work, too.

Archer joined them a short time later, and the meal was a pleasant one. Guinevere wasn't as talkative with her brother around, but she was still mighty pretty. And Archer was full of interesting stories about his quest for butterfly specimens, which had taken him not only all across the country but also to foreign nations as well, including several in South America, where, according to him, the most beautiful butterflies were to be found.

Longarm wasn't really interested in the fluttery critters, but he listened to Archer's stories anyway. When the meal was over, Archer stretched and yawned and said, "This day has been a busy one, and I'm tired. I believe I'll go upstairs and turn in early. Are you coming up, Guin?"

She shook her head. "I'm not ready to go to sleep yet. I thought I might take a walk, since it's a nice evening."

"I'm not sure that's a wise idea," Archer said with a frown. "As we've seen for ourselves, this settlement has its fair share of rough characters."

"Yes, but a woman is supposed to be safe on the frontier. At least, that's what we've been told."

"I know, I know, but—"

Guinevere turned to Longarm and suggested, "Perhaps Mr. Parker would be so kind as to accompany me and see to it that I'm safe?"

Having seen the way Guinevere looked at him from time to time with interest in her eyes, Longarm was halfway expecting something like that. The prospect appealed to him, so he nodded and said, "I'd be glad to, ma'am."

Guinevere turned back to her brother and said, "Mr. Parker strikes me as quite competent, so you see, you don't have to worry about me, Roy."

"Well, all right," Archer said. "But don't remain out too late. We'll be setting out on our search again early in the morning."

"Of course." She stood up and leaned over to plant a kiss on his cheek. "Sleep well, dear."

Longarm had gotten to his feet when Guinevere did. They linked arms again and walked out of the dining room. Even though Guinevere kept a respectable distance between them, and the only things touching were their arms, Longarm enjoyed the contact. He sensed the warmth coming from her body.

"What is it you do, Custis?" she asked as they left the hotel and started to stroll down the street. "Or is it considered impolite out here to ask such a question?"

"Some gents might take it that way, but I don't. I drift, mostly. Work when I have to. I can make a hand on a ranch, and I'm a pretty good gambler. I can drive a stagecoach or a freight wagon. There's always something I can do when I need money."

"So what it amounts to is that you're a vagabond?"

He laughed. "I've been called a heap of things in my life, but I don't believe I've ever been called a vagabond before. Reckon it fits, though."

Greenwood was small enough so that it didn't take them long to walk from one end of it to the other. As they approached the hotel again, Longarm said, "I think we've seen it all."

"Not quite." Guinevere came to a stop in the dark mouth of the alley that ran alongside the hotel, and since the big lawman's arm was still linked with hers, Longarm had to stop, too. As he turned toward her, she went on in a quiet voice, "I'd really like for you to kiss me now, Custis."

Longarm had been expecting *that*, too, and since he didn't like to refuse any reasonable request from a lady, he obliged her. He rested his hands on her shoulders and leaned down as she tilted her head back. Even though it was too dark where they were to see very well, their instincts served them just fine and brought their lips together.

The kiss was gentle at first but grew more urgent. Guinevere moved closer to him so that he felt the soft mounds of her breasts pressing against his chest. Her mouth tasted sweet and seemed to be getting hotter by the second.

Her lips parted as Longarm's tongue probed them. His tongue slid into her mouth to duel and dance with hers. A soft moan of passion came from deep in Guinevere's throat.

When they broke the kiss, she said, "Custis, what would you say if I were to ask you to take me up to your room with you? Would you think me terribly brazen?"

Longarm cupped a hand under her chin and pressed his lips to hers again. "I'd say I like brazen ladies," he replied. "I like 'em just fine."

Chapter 12

For the second time in two days, Matt O'Hara regained consciousness on the bunk inside the Reynolds's soddy. And also for the second time, he found himself looking up into Claire's pretty face.

"So, the owlhoot's awake again," she said.

Matt closed his eyes and tried to ignore the feeling of despair that swept over him. It wouldn't do any good to give in to such things, or he would have done so a long time before now.

He opened his eyes and started to sit up, still intending to leave like they wanted him to. But Claire put a hand on his shoulder, and he was so weak that she had no trouble holding him down.

"Take it easy," she told him. "When you fell earlier, you busted open that wound in your side and lost some more blood. I had to clean it up again and change the bandages, and I don't mind telling you, I'm getting pretty damned tired of it."

He glared at her and asked, "How come a girl like you cusses like a muleskinner?"

"Hell, you haven't even heard me start to cuss yet," she

shot back. "Anyway, you're a fine one to talk. I'd rather cuss than go around robbing banks and shooting people."

"Pap told you, did he?" Matt asked, his face grim.

"What'd you expect? Of course he told me. I got a right to know what sort of fella we're helping, don't I?"

"Well, then, for your information, I didn't rob that bank, and I didn't mean to shoot anybody."

"You went into the bank to rob it, didn't you?"

Matt didn't say anything.

"And a bullet doesn't care whether you meant to fire it or not," she went on. "A fella who gets killed by it is just as dead either way."

"I don't *know* that he's dead."

"You don't know that he's not."

Matt looked away. He couldn't deny what she was saying.

"Anyway," Claire continued, "Pap said you tried to tell him some crazy yarn about how you had to do it to save your ranch, because some woman left you at the altar."

"We didn't get as far as the altar. Abigail called off our engagement before we ever even got close to the church."

Claire used her foot to draw a three-legged stool closer to the bunk. She sat down on it with her trouser-clad legs spread and clasped her hands together between her knees. "How come she broke it off?" she asked. "You treat her bad? Or did she just decide that you couldn't pleasure her good enough in bed?"

Matt stared at her for a second before he burst out, "Good Lord, girl, you shouldn't be talking like that!"

Claire shrugged, unconcerned by his reaction. "You reckon I don't know what goes on between a man and a woman? I may be young, but I ain't ignorant."

"Too young!" Matt said.

"The hell you say! I'm nineteen. Be twenty in two months. By the time my ma was that age, she'd already had me and my little brother who got took by the fever when he was five years old. Most gals are married and have kids by

100

the time they're nineteen, and if they're not, at least they've been behind the barn a few times with some fellas."

Matt turned his head so he was looking at the wall instead of Claire. From her tone of voice, he thought it was pretty clear that she *hadn't* been behind the barn with anybody yet.

"Where's Pap?" he asked between gritted teeth.

"Out tending to the crops, and when he's finished with that, he's gonna take his rifle and see if he can bag a prairie chicken or something like that before it gets dark. We can use some fresh meat."

So he was alone with her, Matt thought. He didn't like the sound of that, given the mood she seemed to be in.

"You're awful touchy about things, for an owlhoot," she said. "I figure a varmint like you must have a saloon girl in every town you've ever been to."

"I'm not an owlhoot," he said, even though he knew it wouldn't do any good, "and for the past five years I've been settled down in the same place, working from can to can't to get my ranch established. The only times I've set foot in a saloon were just to drink a quick beer, and the only lady I've had anything to do with was Abigail, who I never mistreated, at least as far as I know."

"Must not have satisfied her, either, or she wouldn't have called off the engagement."

"Maybe we decided to wait until we were married," he grated.

Claire stared at him and then burst out with a long laugh. "*She* decided, is what you mean. Poor son of a bitch. I reckon doing without like that would be enough to make a man turn owlhoot all by itself."

Matt looked at her and said, "I thought you didn't like me."

"I *don't* like you. You're an outlaw. You may not be a Hell Rider, but you might be just as bad."

"Then why are you acting like this?"

"Like what?" she asked, all mock innocence.

"Like you're trying to . . . trying to . . ." His voice dropped to a whisper. "Seduce me."

She stared at him for a long second before exclaiming, "Seduce you! Good Lord!"

Shame and embarrassment washed over him. He turned his head away again and choked out, "I'm sorry. I reckon I shouldn't have said that."

"You're plumb loco, that's all. I guess it's been too much for you, falling off your horse, getting shot, busting that wound open again . . . all of that. It's made your brain all muddled."

"I reckon so," Matt said. "Still, there's no excuse—"

"Anyway," Claire broke in, "even if I wanted to romp with you, which is unlikely what with your being an outlaw and all, you're too weak to do much. Otherwise, I could have my way with you, and you couldn't stop me."

He wished she would just shut up and go away.

Instead, she said, "Why, if I took a mind to, I could reach under that sheet and start playing with your privates, now couldn't I?"

He moved a hand as if to shield himself from her.

"Oh, don't get all shy on me now. Who do you think pulled all your clothes off of you to tend to that wound?"

"Just my shirt," he said.

Claire smiled and shook her head. "You had so much blood all over you I couldn't tell how many times you'd been hit. I had to strip you right down to the buff to check for other wounds." She laughed. "I got me an eyeful, even though we were so shook up by everything that I don't figure I really appreciated it at the time. Makes me want to look again."

"I bet Pap'll be back any minute," Matt said, a hint of desperation in his voice.

"No, he won't. I know him a heap better'n you do. He'll be out hunting for at least another hour." She scooted the stool closer to the bed. "Plenty of time for us to play around a mite."

"You said I was too weak."

"Well, hell, you don't have to do anything except lay there." She had hold of the sheet. Now that she had decided to take action, she was bold about it. She tugged the sheet all the way down and reached for the buttons of his trousers.

Matt ground his teeth together. This little minx was the one who was loco. One minute she hated and distrusted him because she thought he was an outlaw, the next she was scrambling to get inside his drawers. He told himself to push her hands away. He was strong enough to do *that*, anyway.

But it had been a long time since he'd had anything frisky to do with a woman. Abigail had let him kiss her a little—when she was in the mood, which wasn't all that often, come to think of it—and once he had gotten a couple of fingers on her left breast before she made him stop and told him he was a horrible monster. The look of eager, almost innocent anticipation on Claire's face put a constriction in Matt's chest that had nothing to do with how tight those bandages were wrapped around him.

She had his buttons undone and his trousers spread open. Her fingers hooked in the waistband of his long underwear and dragged it down far enough so that she could reach inside, grab hold of his stiffening shaft, and haul it out. His manhood sprang upright as she freed it. The warm touch of her hand made it finish growing erect.

"Yep," she said with a smile. "That's a nice one, all right."

"How would you know?" he said.

She turned her head so she could look at him. Mischief sparkled in her brown eyes. "I've seen one or two in my time. I may not have done the actual deed before, but you ain't the first fella I've ever played with, Matt O'Hara."

"Yeah, you're a real wanton," he muttered.

Both of her hands tightened around his shaft. "I'll show you," she said as she started pumping up and down on it.

"Good Lord!" he said as he winced in pain. "You're not milking a cow!"

"You hush! I know what I'm doing."

But she slowed down and took it a little easier on him, sliding her hands along the stiff organ. After a minute she delved deeper with one hand and cupped his balls in her palm.

"They're sort of hairy and wrinkled, ain't they?" she said as she lifted them into view.

"Thought you'd seen things like that before," he managed to say.

"I have, I have. You just lay there and be quiet."

His hips gave an involuntary twitch or two as she continued to caress him.

"Be still!" she told him. "You go to jumping around, you'll bust that bullet hole open *again*."

Matt closed his eyes and tried to control his breathing and heart rate. It didn't help much. "It's hard for a fella to . . . stay still," he said, "when a gal is . . . doing things like that . . . to him."

"Oh? How about this?" She wrapped both hands around his shaft again, leaned forward, and ran her tongue around the head of it.

Matt tipped his head back and gritted his teeth hard to keep from hollering.

"Like that, do you?" Claire asked. "Well, I'll just do it again."

She proceeded to lick all the way down one side of his shaft to the base, then moved around and licked her way back up to the top. When she got there, she opened her lips wide and took the head of it into her mouth.

Matt didn't know whether to believe her about her experience, or lack thereof, but even if she had never done this before, she was demonstrating a considerable amount of natural talent at it. She continued pumping slowly with her hands as she sucked. Matt felt the need for release building inside him and knew it was only a matter of time until he exploded. He didn't figure she would want him to do that while she had him in her mouth, so he lifted a shaking hand and put it on her head.

"Claire," he said, his voice thick. "Claire, you better stop."

She lifted her head, making his manhood pop out of her mouth. He couldn't help but feel a twinge of loss and disappointment at the situation.

"Why do you want me to stop?" she asked. "Don't you like it?"

"I like it just fine," he said. "I like it a lot. But if you keep that up I'm going to . . . you know . . . uh, spend my seed in your, uh, in your . . ."

"Ohhhh. I understand." She nodded. "Maybe it'd be better to wait until another time for that." She looked at the throbbing pole of male flesh jutting up from his groin. "But we can't just leave you like that. I reckon that'd be painful."

"You don't know," he said.

"Well, we'll just take care of it another way. Hang on." She grabbed the base of his organ with her left hand and went back to work pumping and stroking with the right. A smile curved her lips.

My God, Matt thought. *She's humming*.

So she was. She must have been enjoying her work. It didn't last long, though, because with a soft, strangled cry, Matt's hips lifted from the bunk again and his climax began to spurt from him. Claire lifted her head to watch and her lips rounded into an impressed O as the thick white drops of fluid shot high into the air. She held on to him with both hands as he shuddered and spent again and again.

"Is it always like that?" she asked when he was finished at last.

Matt's heart slugged like a locomotive in his chest and his pulse played an anvil chorus inside his skull. He barely heard her question over all that commotion. But he managed a weak nod and said, "Just about."

"A mite messy, ain't it?"

"I thought . . . I thought you said . . . you'd played with fellas before."

"Well, yeah, but none of 'em ever got so far as to do that." She wiped up some of his seed from where it had fallen on his belly and rubbed it between her fingertips. "This is the stuff you shoot out when you're inside a girl?"

"Yeah."

"It's hot. Bet it feels pretty good."

"So I've heard tell," Matt said.

"Don't think I'm going to do *that* with you. You're still an outlaw, and Pap doesn't want anything to do with you. Fact is, he wants you to leave as soon as you're able." She smiled down at him. "But I won't let him run you off until you've healed up some. That wouldn't be right." Her voice dropped to a conspiratorial tone. "Anyway, I reckon there's a few more things we can do together without, well, you know. I overheard these two ladies talking once, and one of them said her husband liked to stick his tongue up into her lady parts. She seemed to like it, too. That sounds interesting. Oh, well. Guess we better get you cleaned up before Pap gets back. Wouldn't want him to see any signs of what went on. He might get all riled up."

Matt didn't know whether to laugh or cry, so he settled for closing his eyes and trying to figure out if maybe he had just dreamed the whole thing.

It was real, he decided as Claire went about her business. She was humming again, as happy as a lark.

Chapter 13

The Greenwood Hotel had a set of rear stairs on the outside of the building, which meant that Longarm and Guinevere were able to reach the second-floor hallway without being seen going up together. Longarm led her straight to his room and unlocked the door with a key he took from his pocket, checking first with a glance to see that the matchstick he had wedged between the door and the jamb earlier was still there. It was, so he knew no one had entered the room while he was gone.

When they were inside, he eased the door shut and dropped the key on a dressing table where a lamp had been left burning with the wick trimmed low. She stepped over to Longarm, who took her in his arms and kissed her again.

It was a long, passionate kiss, and when it was over he was fully aroused. She reached down between them to caress the hard, thick shaft through his denim trousers. "My word, Custis," she exclaimed in a soft voice. "You're very well-endowed."

"The Good Lord was generous to me when it came to some things," Longarm admitted. "Might've stubbed His toe when He was pouring in the mule-headedness, though."

Guinevere laughed. "I like a stubborn man. He gets

what he wants most of the time." She trailed a fingertip along the line of his jaw. "What do *you* want, Custis?"

"I reckon you know," he growled, then brought his mouth down on hers again.

They spent the next few minutes kissing, caressing, and undressing each other. With each bit of clothing that fell away, with each smooth-skinned feature revealed by the soft yellow glow of the lamp, Longarm was more impressed with this young woman's sleek, sensual figure. When the last garment was gone and Guinevere stood nude before him, she reached up and unpinned the upswept blond curls, letting them fall thick and loose over her bare shoulders. Some of the strands reached her breasts and teased the dark brown nipples that crowned those soft globes of creamy female flesh. Longarm felt her hair tickle his face as he cupped her breasts and leaned down to flick his tongue against each pebbled nipple in turn.

Guinevere sighed in pleasure and stroked his head as he sucked her nipples into his mouth and laved them with his tongue. His hands slid along the graceful curve of her hips and then stole around to squeeze the rounded cheeks of her derriere. He moved his lips from her breasts to the flat plane of her belly, his tongue trailing a hot path downward. When he reached the triangle of fair, silky hair at the juncture of her thighs, he buried his face in it. Guinevere put her hands on his head and thrust her pelvis against him. A soft cry escaped from her lips.

Longarm rose to his feet and steered her backward toward the bed. When the edge of the mattress hit the back of her knees, she went over without hesitation, sprawling on top of the covers and opening her legs wide.

"Oh, yes, Custis," she gasped. "Keep doing . . . what you were doing."

He had a better angle on the situation now, he thought as he knelt between her thighs and used his thumbs to spread the folds of her sex. Leaning over, he speared his tongue into her, running it up and down her moist opening and lingering at the top to give some special attention to the sensitive area there. As he licked and probed, he raised his head enough to glance upward and look past her upthrust breasts. He saw that Guinevere's eyes were closed and she was jerking her head back and forth as waves of passion rippled through her. He felt the quivering all the way down her soft belly to the core of her being.

Her hips began to thrust, and he knew her culmination had her in its grip. Her thighs pressed hard against his ears. He dug his hands into her rump, as she began to buck. The thumb of his right hand found the puckered brown hole between her cheeks. It was drenched with her juices that had mixed with his spit and run down from her other opening, so he slipped his thumb inside it.

A fresh spasm jolted through Guinevere. Longarm heard an odd sound and looked up to see that she had grabbed one of the pillows from the head of the bed and pressed it to her face so that it muffled the screams of ecstasy welling up her throat. Otherwise she would have woken everybody else in the hotel—and maybe even in the graveyard down the street.

As her shudders began to die away, Longarm gave her a few more licks and kisses and withdrew his thumb. With the pillow still lying over her face, Guinevere sprawled there across the bed, the rapid rise and fall of her chest mute testimony to how worked up she had been.

Longarm pushed himself up beside her and took the pillow away from her face, which was flushed and beaded with sweat. Her eyes were closed and her mouth was slack. She drew in a deep, shuddery breath, then another. Her eyes opened and seemed to have trouble focusing for a moment before her gaze locked in on him. He smiled down at her.

She reached up and caught hold of his head, jerking it down so that she could mash her mouth hard against his.

She didn't seem to care that his lips and tongue were coated with her own juices. She kissed him with an urgency that surged through both of them.

When she drew her head back at last, she put her hands on his shoulders and urged him to lie down. "Now you," she said with a smile.

Longarm wasn't going to argue with that.

She moved around beside him, her long blond hair brushing against his groin as she leaned over his burgeoning shaft. She traced its long, thick contours with a fingertip and said, "I don't know how much of this beautiful beast I can get in my mouth, Custis. I'm not even sure how much of it I can get in my body. But I fully intend to try my best."

He stroked a sleek, warm flank and told her, "I reckon that's all anybody could ask."

She smiled at him and bent to the task.

Over the next few minutes, he discovered just how fluent in French she really was. She did plenty of licking and kissing and squeezing before she opened her mouth wide and engulfed the head of his manhood. She sucked gently while at the same time caressing the heavy sacs at its base. Longarm closed his eyes and heaved a sigh of pleasure.

Guinevere kept it up until Longarm thought he was going to explode from the exquisite sensations she aroused in him. Feeling the telltale throbs that told her his seed was about to gush forth, she lifted her head and wasted no time moving into position above him. As she straddled his hips, she said, "Not yet, Custis. Please, not just yet."

"I'll do my best to hold off," he told her, "but if you plan to take this ride, you better be ready to gallop."

She grasped his shaft and brought it to her drenched opening, then lowered herself onto it with a hard thrust of her hips. Longarm thrust up at the same time. She was so wet that he slid all the way into her with no trouble, sheathing the entire length of his manhood.

Guinevere cried out as he hit bottom. She placed her hands on his broad chest, which was matted with thick brown hair, and leaned forward to brace herself as her hips began to pump. In that position, her breasts hung toward him, enticing him. He cupped them, squeezing and kneading and strumming the erect nipples with his thumbs. Then he moved his hands to her hips to help steady her as their mutual pace increased even more. They were moving at a gallop, all right. This horse was a damn runaway.

Neither of them could continue for very long at this fever pitch of arousal. Shudders began to ripple through Guinevere again, and Longarm took that as his cue to drive up into her one last time, as far as he could go, and unleash his own climax.

By the time he had finished throbbing and spurting and filling her to overflowing, she was on the down side of the slope herself and sagged forward with a long sigh to sprawl on his chest. Her breasts flattened against him. Longarm felt the pounding of her heart, and he figured she could feel his, too. Both of them had given it their all.

They were too sated and out of breath to speak for several minutes. All they could do was hold each other. Then Guinevere managed to say, "Custis, that . . . that was magnificent. Better even than I dared to dream."

A tired chuckle came from Longarm. "We fit together pretty well, all right."

She lifted her head to gaze down at him. "Next time, I want you to be on top," she said.

"There's going to be a next time?"

"Did you ever doubt it?" she asked.

As a matter of fact, he hadn't.

They made love twice more before dozing off at last. Given the long day that had come before and his exertions after supper, no one would have blamed Longarm for falling into a deep, dreamless sleep.

But despite all that, a part of his brain remained alert, as it often did, and late in the night, something disturbed his light slumber. As he opened his eyes, he didn't know if something in the room had awakened him, or if it was just his thoughts nagging at him. The lamp had guttered out earlier, leaving the room in darkness. He didn't hear any movement, and Guinevere was still sleeping beside him, her breathing deep and regular. He reached over anyway to the bedside table and closed his hand around the butt of his Colt, which he had placed in easy reach before going to sleep.

Long moments passed as he lay there, motionless now and in utter silence. His keen senses searched the darkness, alert for any threat. Only when he was satisfied that he and Guinevere were alone in the room and there was no danger lurking did Longarm relax.

But that still left him with the question of what had awakened him. Being careful not to awaken Guinevere, he slid out of the bed and padded barefoot over to the hotel room's single window. A little light filtered into the room through the narrow opening between the curtains.

Longarm's clothes were on a chair beside the window. He reached down, found his shirt, and slipped a three-for-a-nickel cheroot out of the pocket. He put it in his mouth and left it unlit, then pushed one of the curtains back to widen the gap between them.

The window looked down on Greenwood's main street. The glass had been raised several inches to let some fresh air into the room. That aperture allowed sounds to penetrate, too, although at this time of night the settlement was pretty quiet. Longarm heard faint strains of music coming from the Double Diamond. All the other saloons appeared to have closed down for the night.

He heard hoofbeats and the jingle of bit chains, too, and as he stood there a group of riders moved past in the street. Dim light from the night lamp in the hotel lobby spilled through the windows and illuminated the scene enough for Longarm to be able to make out the faces of several of the men. He stiffened as he recognized two of them.

The hard case called Abilene—and Dog McCluskey.

Longarm had seen McCluskey with Abilene and the other hired guns earlier in the evening. Now there was no doubt that the Dog was part of their bunch. That was something of a departure for McCluskey, who had always played a lone hand in his career as a desperado rather than operating with a gang. But maybe the Dog had gotten lonesome and decided to throw in with a pack of similar curs.

Another question tugged at Longarm's brain. Where the hell were they going at this time of night?

He was willing to bet that whatever they were up to, it wasn't anything good.

He grimaced as he stood there, the wheels of his brain clicking over, and then with the cheroot still clenched between his teeth he reached for his clothes and began pulling them on. Wasting no time, he got dressed, buckled the cross-draw rig around his lean hips, and settled his hat on his head. Guinevere hadn't stirred, and her sleep seemed to be as sound as ever.

Longarm opened the door and cat-footed out of the room, easing it shut behind him. The hotel had a shed and corral out back where he had put his horse earlier, so he headed for the rear stairs.

He needed only a few minutes to get his McClellan saddle on the horse. He had noted that the riders were headed west as they left town, so he rode in that direction himself. The night was dark, with only a thin sliver of moon and the usual scattering of stars. That was both a blessing and a curse. The darkness would make it more difficult for him to trail McCluskey and the others, but it would also keep them from spotting him.

Longarm reined his horse to a stop at the edge of town and listened. He heard hoofbeats coming from ahead of him and knew he was on the right track. The riders were moving faster now that they had left the settlement behind, so Longarm put his mount into an easy lope that ate up the ground. He would need to be careful not to get too close to his quarry. With luck, the hoofbeats of their own horses would cover up any sounds of pursuit.

It wouldn't take the gunmen long to reach the broad valley where Pap and Claire Reynolds and the other homesteaders had established their farms. Ever since Longarm had seen the riders leaving town, he'd had a sneaking suspicion that was where they were headed. As he rode toward the top of the long rise that overlooked the valley, he slowed his horse to a walk and then a halt. He heard the hoofbeats of the horses he was following as they came to a stop as well. Men's voices spoke, but they were so faint he couldn't make out any of the words.

Longarm swung down from the saddle, leaving his mount ground-hitched. He stole forward on foot. His right hand hovered near the butt of his Colt. A line of brush gave him some cover, although he had to be careful not to make any noise as he moved through it. He tested each step before he let his weight down on his foot, lest a stray twig crack underneath him and warn the men he was sneaking up on.

He wasn't sure why they had paused, but a moment later he found out. Even though it was muffled somehow, a harsh voice he recognized as belonging to Abilene said, "All right, if everybody's ready, let's go."

They spurred their horses forward. Longarm stiffened and crouched in the brush as he realized that the gang of gunmen was closer than he had thought, almost right on top of him, as a matter of fact. The hoofbeats of their horses filled the air like thunder. Longarm parted some of the brush to peer out at them as they galloped past him, less than forty feet away.

114

And damned if it wasn't true, he saw with a shock. They had donned long dusters and removed their hats—

And somehow set fire to their heads.

The Hell Riders were on the move.

Chapter 14

Longarm was mule-headed enough not to believe that the heads of the gunmen were actually blazing away like miniature bonfires—but that was sure what it looked like. As the gang surged off into the night, he turned and ran back toward the spot where he had left his horse.

As he pounded through the darkness, he thought about what he had seen, not wanting to believe the evidence of his own eyes. Pap Reynolds had mentioned that Claire thought the Hell Riders were just men, that those flaming heads were a trick of some sort. Longarm knew for a fact they were men, because he had seen them leave Greenwood and followed them out here to the homesteaders' valley.

But how had they transformed themselves into the creatures he had seen? He couldn't answer that one.

He could damn sure trail them and find out what they were going to do, though.

His horse hadn't strayed. The hostler at the stable where Longarm had rented it back in Denver before setting out on this assignment had sworn the animal was trained to stay ground-hitched, and so far that claim had proven to be true. He mounted up and hurried after the Hell Riders, not bothering to be quiet about it now. The way they had galloped off in such a rush, they wouldn't know he was behind them. Anyway, they were concentrating on whatever grim errand had brought them out here.

Before Longarm caught up to them, he heard the sudden crackle of gunfire in the night. Just as he had expected, the Hell Riders were attacking one of the farms in the valley. It wasn't the Reynolds place this time, but that didn't matter. Longarm knew he had to help the settlers.

Anyway, Dog McCluskey was one of the gang, so that meant the trouble in these parts was now part of Longarm's official business after all.

He pulled his Winchester from the saddle sheath and leaned forward over the neck of the horse as he urged the animal to greater speed. The scattered gunshots were picking up in frequency and intensity. A real corpse-and-cartridge session was under way, somewhere up ahead.

Flying through the darkness, Longarm's horse topped a rise, kicking up clods of dirt as its hooves pounded the earth. Longarm saw spurts of orange flame and recognized them as muzzle flashes. He saw the burning heads of the Hell Riders, too. They were every bit as garish as the gun blasts.

The raiders were galloping around a soddy, pouring lead into the humble dwelling. Longarm spotted a wink of fire from inside the homesteader's shack and knew at least one person was in there fighting back. The odds were stacked in favor of the Hell Riders, though. There were at least a dozen of them.

Longarm took in the situation in little more time than a heartbeat. He hauled back on the reins and brought his horse to a stop. The range was about two hundred yards, not that far for a Winchester under better conditions, but it was dark and his targets were galloping around, constantly on the move. It would take some mighty fancy shooting to drop any of them from this distance.

But that was just about the only chance the sodbuster

had, and Longarm knew it. He said to the horse, "Steady, now, old son," and brought the rifle to his shoulder.

A moment later he pressed the trigger, and as the Winchester cracked and kicked against his shoulder he was rewarded by the sight of a blazing head dropping suddenly as the body it was attached to tumbled out of the saddle. Longarm worked the rifle's lever, shifted his aim, and fired again. He wasn't sure if he scored a hit that time, but he didn't waste time worrying about it. The Winchester held fifteen rounds. He started cranking the lever and emptying the rifle as fast as he could.

Now that he had the raiders' attention, they broke off their attack on the soddy, wheeled their horses around, and galloped toward him, just as he had hoped they would. Charging into the middle of the fight wouldn't have done any good. He couldn't have outfought all of the Hell Riders and he knew it. But he had drawn them away from the homesteader's place, and now all he had to do was give them the slip.

Yeah. That was all.

Longarm yanked his mount around and jabbed his boot heels in the animal's flanks. The horse leaped forward. Longarm didn't try to reload the Winchester before he shoved it back in the saddle boot. Speed and stealth were his primary weapons now. Again he bent low and urged the horse to greater speed.

He sure hoped the critter wouldn't step in any of those prairie dog holes he had noticed all over the valley the day before. If the horse fell at this speed, with the Hell Riders hot on their trail, both of them would wind up dead.

Longarm tugged his hat down tighter on his head as the wind of his passage threatened to pluck it off and send it sailing away. A glance over his shoulder told him that his pursuers had thundered over the top of the rise. He saw the blobs of light bobbing along. In the time it had taken them to mill around before they came after him, he had gained fifty or sixty yards. They shouldn't be able to see him at this distance, in the darkness. He didn't want them to give up and go back to attacking the soddy, though, so he slipped his Colt out and triggered three fast shots toward the raiders. The bullets wouldn't hit anything, but the muzzle flashes would tell them where he was so they could keep following him.

As he faced forward again, he plucked fresh cartridges from the loops on his shell belt and replaced the expended rounds in the Colt, thumbing them into the cylinder by feel. He had loaded the weapon so many times that even doing so in near-pitch-darkness on the hurricane deck of a galloping horse didn't present too much difficulty. He reached across his body and holstered the reloaded gun.

A dark line appeared to one side of him, running at an angle. He figured it marked the bushes along a creek, so he veered in that direction. Sure enough, he came to the narrow stream a moment later, forced his horse through the brush and down the bank, and splashed into the creek. He reined to a halt. As he sat there with the horse's sides heaving as it blew, he listened for the sounds of pursuit. He heard hoofbeats not far away, but he couldn't see those burning heads anymore.

Maybe they had put out the fires.

A grimace tugged at the corners of Longarm's mouth under the sweeping mustache. He had been counting on those mysterious fires to warn him if the Hell Riders were closing in on him. The bastards were smart, though. They had realized that the blazes made perfect targets at night.

"Find that son of a bitch," a man's voice called. Longarm thought it was Abilene's. "Whoever he is, I want him dead!"

"Better pipe down," another man advised, "or he'll put a bullet through you just like he did Baker."

"Yeah, yeah," Abilene muttered, but he shut up and so did the other man.

Longarm drew his gun without making a sound. He waited, holding the horse close against the brush-covered bank of the stream. Long minutes passed as the Hell Riders continued to search for whoever had interrupted their attack on the soddy. For a harrowing few moments, two of them rode up and down the stream less than fifty yards from Longarm, but neither of them spotted him and his mount against the darkness of the brush.

Somebody let out a piercing whistle. The raiders converged on the spot. They held a low-voiced conversation. Longarm strained his ears but could understand only part of what was being said.

". . . go back to that damn sodbuster's . . ."

"No . . . already put . . . fear of God in him . . . pull out if he . . . what's good for him."

". . . about that other hombre . . ."

". . . must've got away . . . wish we knew who he was . . ."

". . . sure to tell . . . about it. Maybe he'll know who . . ."

Longarm gritted his teeth together in frustration. He had a feeling that one of the Hell Riders had just said that he would tell their boss about what had happened. Longarm had a feeling the varmint might have even named the man behind the Hell Riders. The homesteaders thought that Carlton Barstow was responsible for the raids, but so far Longarm hadn't seen any evidence of that one way or the other.

Hoofbeats that began to dwindle in the distance told him the Hell Riders were moving on. He would have tried to follow them, but he could tell they were splitting up, spreading out over the countryside. They would make their way back to Greenwood by ones and twos, so that folks wouldn't associate them with the gang that had raided the soddy.

Longarm waited until they were gone before leaving the creek and riding up onto the bank. He had mixed emotions about this night's work. He was glad he had disrupted the attack on the homesteader's place, but he was frustrated that he hadn't been able to get a better line on the culprit behind the trouble around here. Also, he wasn't any closer to capturing Dog McCluskey than he had been when he started out, and that was his real job.

But Longarm knew better than to kid himself. He might not have a tail, but he, too, was like a dog in some ways. Once he had sunk his teeth into a mystery, like that of the Hell Riders, he didn't want to let go.

Besides, he wanted to help Pap and Claire and the other homesteaders, so they wouldn't have to live in fear of those grotesque night riders.

He had just turned his horse to head back to Greenwood when the brush crackled behind him and a voice called, "Don't move, damn you! I figured you were still around here somewhere, that's why I sent the others on and waited. Get those hands up!"

Longarm froze, knowing the words would be backed up by a leveled six-gun. He knew, too, that the voice belonged to Abilene and that he couldn't expect any mercy from the burly gunman. He dropped the reins and brought his hands up to shoulder level, dipping for a second into his shirt pocket with the left one as he did so. From behind him, Abilene couldn't see that move.

"Take it easy, old son," Longarm said. "I don't know what's going on here, but I don't mean you no harm."

"What are you gonna do, claim that you ain't the man who shot at us a little while ago?" The sneer in Abilene's voice was plain. "I know better. Nobody else would be wanderin' around out here at night except the man who horned in on our play."

"What play was that?" Longarm asked. "Setting your

122

heads on fire and attacking the farm of some poor sodbuster who just wants to make a living for him and his family?"

A harsh laugh came from Abilene. "You don't know the half of it, mister." He paused. "Say, there's somethin' familiar about your voice. I've got it now! You're the bastard who helped the Reynolds girl. You just can't help mixin' in with things that are none of your business, can you?"

"All right," Longarm said. "You got me. Better take me to your boss so he can figure out what to do with me." It was a long shot that Abilene would follow the suggestion and reveal the mastermind's identity, but it didn't hurt to try.

Instead, the gunman laughed and said, "I'm gonna take you to the boss, all right. But you'll be dead when I deliver you!"

Longarm heard the finality in Abilene's tone and knew he had run out of time. He made the only play he had remaining to him.

His thumb snapped the head of the match he had palmed from his pocket. The lucifer flared into life. With the same motion, Longarm flung the burning match out to the side. As he had hoped, the sudden glare distracted Abilene and drew his eyes as he squeezed the trigger, so that his aim was off and the bullet whined through the air to the left of Longarm's head.

The big lawman had already eased his boots out of the stirrups. Even as Abilene fired, missing to the left, Longarm went to the right, pitching out of the saddle. His gun was in his hand before he hit the ground. He rolled over as Abilene fired again. This slug kicked up dirt near Longarm's head but was still a clean miss. On his belly, Longarm tipped up the barrel of the Colt and triggered twice.

As best he could in the darkness and the heat of the moment, he had aimed low, hoping to hit Abilene somewhere in the body and disable him without killing him right away. He wanted answers to some questions.

But the gunman's horse spooked and reared up, and that changed the angle of Longarm's shots. Abilene flipped backward out of the saddle as if someone had just swatted him with a giant club. He landed with a hard *thud* as his horse danced off to the side.

Longarm pushed himself to his hands and knees and then came to his feet, keeping his gun trained on the dark shape sprawled on the ground. Using caution, he approached Abilene. The man wasn't moving, and no sound came from him. The starlight showed Longarm a dark pool spreading around his head.

Longarm struck another match, and by its light he saw that one of his bullets had struck Abilene in the throat, tearing through it and angling on up through his brain to explode out the top of his skull. It was an ugly sight, but one that left no doubt Abilene was dead.

Longarm listened for hoofbeats, in case some of the other Hell Riders had heard the shots and were coming back to investigate. The night was quiet, though. He replaced the spent cartridges, holstered the gun, and knelt beside the corpse to go through Abilene's pockets.

He didn't find anything except makings for a smoke, a few coins, a roll of bills, and a greasy deck of cards with pictures of naked ladies painted on them. There was nothing to indicate who Abilene and the other Hell Riders worked for. Longarm pocketed the money, left the cards and tobacco. He stood up and walked toward Abilene's horse, holding out a hand and talking in a soft voice to the skittish animal. He wanted to check Abilene's saddlebags.

It took a little patience, but after a few minutes he got close enough to catch hold of the dangling reins. The horse settled down then, as soon as it felt the touch of a firm human hand. Longarm patted the animal on the shoulder and moved along its flank. He opened the left-hand saddlebag and thrust his hand in, finding nothing except a box of ammunition, a flask that gurgled a little when he shook it, and something wrapped in paper that turned out to be a stale biscuit. Disappointed, he murmured to the horse and moved around to check the other saddlebag. He undid the catch on the leather flap, reached inside—

And pulled out a handful of fire.

Chapter 15

His hand wasn't burning, of course. In fact, as soon as he felt the thing, he realized it was a hood of some sort, made of cloth that could be pulled over the head.

But it glowed in the dark like it was on fire, and it was large and baggy so that when Longarm shook it, the light it gave off looked like dancing flames.

He grinned. Claire Reynolds had been right. It was a trick, pure and simple. Well, maybe not so simple. There were quite a few things in nature that glowed on their own. Phosphorescence, it was called, Longarm remembered.

But nothing natural was quite this bright and flamelike. Somebody had mixed up some sort of chemical concoction and permeated the hoods of the Hell Riders with it. In the darkness, it had looked like their heads were ablaze. Whoever had come up with this, the hombre was plenty smart.

Longarm felt around in the saddlebag where he had found the hood but didn't discover anything else. He cached the hood in one of his own saddlebags and fastened it. Then, leaving Abilene's body where it lay, he saddled up and headed for Greenwood.

The hour was well after midnight by the time he

reached the settlement. He unsaddled his horse, turned it into the corral behind the hotel, and stowed his saddle in the shed. He took the saddlebags with him, draping them over his shoulder, but he didn't enter the hotel right away. Instead, he returned to the corral, slipping through the bars in the pole fence and approaching the seven or eight horses who were penned there. Murmuring in a soothing voice so they wouldn't get spooked, he inspected the animals as best he could, running his hand along the flanks of several of them. Satisfied with what he had found, he left the corral and climbed the rear steps to the second-floor landing. The hallway was dim and deserted when he slipped inside.

Guinevere Archer was still asleep in his bed, but she woke up when he slid in beside her. He had taken off all his clothes, and his hope was that she wouldn't even realize he had been gone.

She turned toward him, not fully awake yet but aware enough of their shared nudity that she reached down between them and closed her hand around his thick manhood. Right away, he began to stiffen at her touch. She gave a pleased but sleepy murmur and began to stroke the hardening shaft.

"You're insatiable, do you know that, Custis?"

"If that means I can't get enough of you, that's sure right," Longarm told her. He found one of her breasts in the darkness, cupped it, and thumbed the nipple. She snuggled closer to him and kissed him.

Then she rolled over so that she faced away from him and whispered, "Take me from behind."

Longarm spooned with her, putting his arms around her, and slipped his organ into her. They made slow, sleepy, sensuous love, and this time when Guinevere's climax washed over her, she didn't scream. She just gave a long, deep sigh of pleasure instead.

It was a fitting end to an eventful, informative night, Longarm thought.

• • •

Guinevere left his bed before dawn, slipping out after giving him a kiss and whispering an endearment. Longarm figured she wouldn't want her brother to discover she wasn't in her room and wonder where she had been all night if she stayed. Once she was gone, he rolled over and slept for another couple of hours.

When he woke up again, he got dressed and went downstairs for breakfast, putting himself on the outside of a large plate full of flapjacks and bacon, washed down with a pot of strong black coffee. Feeling pretty good, he stepped outside onto the hotel porch.

The sound of angry voices caught his attention right away. Trouble had come to Greenwood this time.

Longarm looked along the street toward a squat, stone building that he had noticed the day before when he was looking around the settlement. It housed the office of Marshal Tom Reeder.

Often when Longarm entered a town on business, he would stop and inform the local law of his presence, but based on what he had heard about Marshal Reeder, he hadn't bothered. The man had turned a blind eye to the troubles of the settlers, and in the dispute between Carlton Barstow and the homesteaders, there was a good chance Reeder was on the side of the cattle baron. He had also stated publicly that he wasn't going to arrest Dog McCluskey as long as the outlaw didn't break any laws in Greenwood.

Now several horses were drawn up in front of Reeder's office. One of the riders had dismounted and was talking to the marshal in a loud, blustery voice. The horse with the empty saddle was a big black stallion that Longarm recognized from the day before. He recognized the man who had ridden it into town, too. Carlton Barstow was chewing out a short, stocky, gray-haired man with a badge pinned to his vest who could only be Marshal Tom Reeder.

Curious what this was all about, Longarm ambled closer. When Barstow paused for breath, Reeder said, "I'm mighty sorry to hear about all that, Mr. Barstow, you know I am, but there ain't really anything I can do about it. My jurisdiction ends at the edge of town."

"What sort of self-respectin' lawman is gonna ignore rustlin' and murder because of a thing like that?" Barstow demanded. His face was mottled red with anger, and the contrast with his white hair made his skin look even more flushed.

"I can send word to the county sheriff—" Reeder suggested.

"Hell, it'll take weeks for that son of a bitch to send a deputy over here, if he ever gets around to it! He's about as useless as you are, Reeder."

The local star packer was starting to look mad, too, but he kept it under control. Longarm figured he was used to such high-handed abuse from Barstow.

"I suppose I could ride out there and take a look around," Reeder said. "But even if I find anything, I won't have any legal authority to make an arrest."

"I don't want you to arrest anybody," Barstow said. "The boys and me will take care of everything that needs to be done. You just ride along so if there's ever any question about it, we can say that we had the law with us."

Reeder looked nervous now. "That sounds like vigilante work to me. I can't be part of that, Mr. Barstow. I just can't."

"All right, damn you," the cattleman grated. "Just remember, I tried to do this proper-like. Should've known better. I've been the only real law in these parts for a long time, and I'm damned if that's gonna change now!"

Barstow snatched the reins of his horse from the man holding them, grabbed the horn, and swung up into the saddle. He jerked his mount around and put the spurs to it.

130

With his hard-faced cowboys following closely behind him, he rode out of town, headed west.

Marshal Reeder watched them go with a worried expression on his face. He took off his hat, pulled a bandanna from his pocket, and mopped sweat off his face. The morning was turning warm, but it wasn't *that* warm yet.

Longarm sauntered up to him and said, "Morning, Marshal. Looks like you've got some trouble on your plate."

Reeder glanced at him. "Who the hell are you, mister? I haven't seen you around town before, have I?"

"I just rode into Greenwood yesterday." Longarm decided to go ahead and make a play, since he was starting to have a pretty good idea what was going on around here. "Name's Long." He paused. "Deputy U.S. Marshal Custis Long, out of the Denver office."

Reeder's muddy brown eyes widened in surprise. "A U.S. marshal?" he repeated. "You're a federal lawman?"

"Yeah, but I'd appreciate it if you'd keep that under your hat for now, old son. What say we go in your office and you tell me what put that burr under Carlton Barstow's saddle?"

"You know Mr. Barstow?"

"We've never met," Longarm said, "but I know him when I see him. Looked like he's mighty upset, too."

"Yeah. Yeah, he is." Reeder clutched Longarm's sleeve like a drowning man. "Come on inside. I'll tell you all about it."

The two men went into Reeder's office, which was a typical small-town lawman's lair with a cast-iron stove in the corner, a rack of rifles and shotguns on the wall, and a cell block with two small cells in the back, on the other side of a heavy door that stood open at the moment because the cells were empty.

Reeder looked at the badge and bona fides Longarm showed him, then went behind the scarred desk and said,

"Help yourself to coffee. I can't believe the government sent a U.S. marshal out here to help me."

"You can spit out that particular bite of the apple," Longarm told him. "I wasn't sent here to help you, Reeder. My job is to arrest Dog McCluskey, or if he won't surrender peaceable-like, to take him into custody by force."

The local lawman paled. "McCluskey? You're after the Dog?"

Longarm nodded. He left the coffeepot on the stove, knowing from experience that the brew inside it would be a day or two old, thick as mud, and strong enough to walk off on its own two legs.

"But . . . but McCluskey hasn't broken any laws here in Greenwood," Reeder went on.

"Doesn't matter. He's wanted on federal charges stemming from some stagecoach holdups, and I'm authorized to go wherever I need to in order to arrest him."

"Then you're not after the Hell Riders?"

"I didn't say that." Longarm snagged a ladderback chair, turned it around, and straddled it. As he sat down, he went on, "Even though the trouble around here wasn't part of my original assignment, I'm taking an interest in it because McCluskey's involved."

Reeder looked astonished again. "He is? How?"

Longarm waved off the question and said, "Let me worry about that. For now, tell me what got Barstow so riled up this morning."

Reeder pulled out the bandanna and wiped his face with it again. "Rustlers hit the Boxed B again last night."

"Barstow's lost stock before?"

"He's been complainin' about it for a month now. Wants me to do something about it, but I keep explainin' to him that it's not my jurisdiction."

Longarm nodded. He couldn't really fault Reeder for wanting to honor the legal boundaries of his office as town marshal, but on the other hand, Longarm had always been the sort of star packer who would bend a few rules in order to see justice done. He didn't have much sympathy for a lawman who did things by the book simply because it was easier that way, and that was how he had Marshal Tom Reeder pegged.

"Barstow said something about murder?" Longarm prodded.

"Yeah, when the rustlers hit his place last night, there was some shooting and a couple of his hands were killed. That's the first time anybody's wound up dead." Reeder shook his head. "I knew those damn Hell Riders would kill somebody sooner or later."

Longarm frowned. "Wait a minute. Are you saying the Hell Riders are the ones who rustled Barstow's stock and gunned down his men?"

"Well, yeah, sure. Barstow's blamed 'em right along."

"The homesteaders in the valley just west of here believe that the Hell Riders work for Barstow," Longarm said.

"Yeah, I know. I've had some of them in my office complainin' and tellin' me I've got to do something about it, too. And all the time Barstow's been convinced it's some of those sodbusters who're to blame. He says they're tryin' to get back at him because he's said he wants all of them out of the valley."

Longarm tugged at his earlobe and scraped a thumbnail along his jawline as he thought about what Reeder had just told him, then he nodded. Everything fit together. A few questions were still unanswered, but he figured he could root out the truth once he put a stop to all this ruction.

"What did Barstow plan to do when he rode off from here in such a hurry?"

"He's headed out to the valley to search all those homesteaders' farms," Reeder said. "He wants to see if he can find his missing cows, and if he does, he figures to carry out his own justice on whoever took 'em."

"Are you talking about a lynching party?" Longarm asked, his face grim.

"Be hard to lynch anybody. There ain't no trees out there tall enough for that. I reckon Barstow can think of something else to do to whoever rustled his stock and killed his men, though."

"Those farmers didn't do it," Longarm said as he came to his feet. "Hell, one of their places got hit last night by the Hell Riders."

"You know that for a fact?"

"Saw it with my own eyes," Longarm said.

"But . . . but some of Barstow's men saw the Hell Riders, too! They traded shots with the varmints, and a couple of them got gunned down!"

"That's what Barstow's men *said* happened. Maybe the men who got killed were a couple of hombres who wouldn't go along with the plan anymore. Or maybe they wanted more than their fair share of the profits."

Reeder might not be the bravest lawman in the world, but he wasn't stupid. He grasped what Longarm was getting at and came to his feet.

"You mean some of Barstow's own men are behind the rustlin'?"

"The Hell Riders were busy last night raiding one of those farms in the valley. I guess they could have ridden over to the Boxed B later and raised a ruckus there, too, but I don't think that's what happened. Once the Hell Riders showed up a month ago, some of Barstow's punchers figured they could loot the ranch and the Hell Riders would get the blame. Barstow played right into their hands by jumping to the conclusion that the homesteaders were really the Hell Riders. The rustlers knew that Barstow was liable to blame anything bad on the sodbusters."

Agitated, Reeder raked his fingers through his hair. "You're right, Marshal. Damn it, I can feel it in my gut. You're right. What are you gonna do about it?"

"As mad as Barstow was when he left here, he'll seize any excuse to start wiping out those farmers," Longarm said. "When the farmers fight back, it'll turn into a bloodbath. I can't stand by and let that happen. I'm going to head out there and see if I can't stop it." He turned toward the door and started to stalk out of the office.

Reeder hesitated, then grabbed his hat and said, "Wait up! I'll come with you."

Longarm glanced back. "You sure about that? It's out of your jurisdiction."

Reeder flushed at the sharp, disdainful tone of Longarm's words. "I'm sure," he said as he crammed his hat on his head and then jerked one of the Winchesters out of the rack. He grabbed a box of shells from a desk drawer and started after Longarm. "I don't want any of those sodbusters' blood on my head."

Longarm nodded. "In that case, I'll be glad to have you along, Marshal. Let's ride."

Chapter 16

Just as Claire had predicted, Pap had been out hunting until dusk the day before, and when he came back he had the carcasses of two plump prairie chickens with him. "Fry these up, gal!" he said as he put the bloody, feathered bodies on the table. "We got us some fresh meat!"

Pap hadn't paid much attention to Matt O'Hara, who lay on the bunk with the sheet pulled up over his bandaged chest. Claire had done a good job of cleaning him up so that no sign remained of what she and Matt had done earlier that afternoon. Rather, what she had done *to* Matt, although in the end he had been a willing enough participant, whether he wanted to admit that to himself or not.

Despite Pap's lack of suspicions, Matt felt guilty and kept his head turned toward the wall most of the time so he wouldn't have to look at the old man. It wasn't like he had taken advantage of Pap's innocent little granddaughter, he tried to tell himself. The whole thing had been Claire's idea, and as she had said, he was too weak to stop her from doing whatever she wanted. The misgivings were there anyway.

Matt hoped he would heal up soon and be able to travel again. The longer he stayed around here, the greater the chance that Marshal Chad Haimes would ride up someday and arrest him. And the longer he stayed, the more complicated things with Claire were liable to get, too . . .

He was restless during the night, maybe because he worried that Claire would try to crawl in the bunk with him while Pap was right there in the cabin. From the cool, almost hostile way she treated him, though, no one would have guessed what had gone on. She kept her distance, not only during the night but the next morning, also, and Matt was glad of that.

After breakfast, both Pap and Claire went out to tend to the crops they had growing, leaving Matt alone in the soddy. "Don't steal anything while we're gone," Claire told him as they left.

Matt just looked away. Women were the most baffling creatures in the world. Yesterday afternoon she'd been playing with his talleywhacker like it was the grandest toy in the world, and this morning she acted like she couldn't stand the sight of him. He sighed in despair of understanding women, life, or any other damned thing.

Around midmorning Pap returned to the cabin. "Came back to fill our water bucket," he explained to Matt, "and Claire told me to be sure and come inside to check on you."

"She did?" Matt asked, surprised that she would be so concerned about him.

"Yep. Fact is, you're damned near all she's talked about this mornin', mister." Pap glared at him. "I ain't too happy about it, neither. If I didn't know better, I'd say the gal's done went and gone sweet on you. Thought I raised her better'n to get calf-eyed over an owlhoot."

"You're wrong about her," Matt said. "She hates me. She pretty much told me so, no matter what she said out there while you were working."

"Oh, she still says you ain't nothin' but a low-down, snake-blooded, good-for-nothin' desperado. It's just the *way* she says it that's got me a mite worried."

Matt shook his head. "You don't have anything to worry about. As soon as I get my strength back, I'll be leaving. I appreciate what you folks have done for me, and I won't burden you any longer than I have to."

"Ain't been that much of a burden, I reckon. And you ain't got no horse."

"I'll walk."

"We'll see, we'll see. For now, you just rest. Anything you need before I get back to work?"

"No, I can't think of a—"

The sudden blast of a gunshot, followed by angry shouts, came from outside and made both Matt and Pap jerk their heads toward the open door.

Even though Pap was on his feet to start with and Matt was flat on his back, the older man reached the door only a second before the younger one. Matt had grabbed his shirt on the way and was pulling it on as both of them crowded through the door. They got outside in time to see Claire running toward the soddy with a couple of horsemen pounding along close behind her.

As they watched in shock, one of the cowboys shook out a loop in his lasso and sent it sailing through the air. The horsehide lariat settled over Claire's body. With practiced ease, the cowboy jerked the loop tight, pinning her arms to her sides. Then he hauled back on the reins, bringing his mount to a skidding stop. He had dallied the rope around his saddlehorn, causing it to snap taut and yank Claire off her feet. She cried out as she was slammed to the ground like an unruly calf roped for branding.

The cowboy who had lassoed her must have thought the same thing. Laughing, he called to his companion, "I got her, Bud! Now you can hog-tie her!"

Furious, Pap cried, "We'll see about that!" and started to lift his rifle. Matt caught hold of the barrel and forced the weapon down.

"Hold on, Pap. Those boys aren't alone."

He used his other hand to point toward another group of riders approaching the soddy at a slower pace. Matt recognized the haughty figure of Carlton Barstow leading the way, followed by several more of his punchers. The Boxed B hands were driving four steers in front of them.

"Get that little hellion on her feet and bring her to the soddy," Barstow ordered the man who had roped Claire. Then he came on toward Matt and Pap. His face was set in cold, angry lines.

Barstow didn't have his dander up any more than Pap did, though. Matt glanced over and saw that the old-timer was shaking with rage. "Better settle down, Pap," he warned. "There are too many of them. They'll kill us if you give them any excuse."

"Did you see what they done to Claire?" Pap asked in a tortured voice. "Did you see?"

"I saw," Matt replied, and he found that he was filled with anger, too, as well as worry for Claire. It might have to wait until he got his strength back, but he swore he would settle the score with the puncher who had dabbed a loop on her.

Bud had dismounted and hauled Claire back to her feet. With the rope still tight around her body, she was forced to stumble along toward the soddy. The whole group—Barstow, his men, Claire, and the four steers—came up to the shack and stopped.

With a visible effort at self-control, Pap said, "I done told you before, Barstow, and I'll tell you again. You ain't welcome on my land. And turn my granddaughter a-loose before I blast a hole in you, you mangy buzzard."

Barstow ignored everything Pap had said. Instead of responding to it, he pointed at the steers and said, "You recognize those cows, old man?"

"Why should I?"

"Because they're part of the bunch that you and your polecat friends rustled from my ranch last night!"

140

Pap gaped at him. So did Matt.

When the shock of the accusation started to wear off and Pap regained his voice, he burst out, "That's plumb loco! I never rustled a cow in my whole blasted life!"

"Don't bother lyin'," Barstow said in an icy voice. "We found 'em hidden in a brush corral in that gully not half a mile from here, on land that you been claimin' is yours, Reynolds. I dispute that claim, but you can't dispute the evidence of these cows!"

"I tell you, I never saw the blamed critters before!"

"They're your share of the stock that was stole last night when you and your damn sodbuster friends made yourselves up as the Hell Riders and raided my ranch," Barstow said.

Matt was dizzy from surprise and confusion as much as he was from the aftereffects of that bullet wound. He said, "You're wrong, Barstow. Pap was right here last night. And the Hell Riders have been attacking the farmers, not the other way around."

Barstow turned his cold gaze on the young man. "I still don't know what your part in this is, mister, but I'd advise you to stay out of it. You don't look like a sodbuster, but if you side with them, you'll get the same thing they're gonna get!"

"What're you talkin' about, Barstow?" Pap asked.

"I'm talkin' about tar and feathers," the rancher said. "I'd string up your scrawny carcass from the closest high limb if there was one to be found, but since there ain't, we'll do the next best thing! Two of my men were killed last night, so you and your dirt-grubbin' friends have to pay for that. I'm goin' back to the Boxed B, roundin' up my whole crew, and we're comin' back here to haul out every damned one of you sodbusters and teach you a lesson. We'll burn what we can burn and trample what we can't. Anybody tries to stop us will be shot dead. And by the end of the day, those of you who are left will be on your way out of this valley. If you ever show your faces here again, me and my men will kill you on sight."

It was a long, ugly speech, and Matt didn't want to believe what he was hearing. There was no doubting the resolve on Barstow's rugged face, though. The rancher was taking the law into his own hands, just as he had done on countless occasions when he'd first settled here decades earlier. When word got out of such an atrocity, it might bring in outside lawmen or even the army, but of course by then it would be too late to help Pap and Claire and all the other homesteaders.

"You can't do that," Matt said. "You just can't."

"Who's gonna stop me?" Barstow demanded. "An old man? A hellion of a girl? A shot-up drifter?"

Sobbing, Claire said, "I tried to stop 'em, Pap. I got off a shot, but I missed."

Barstow gestured to some of his cowboys. "Take the old man."

Matt moved in front of Pap and said, "Pap didn't do anything, I tell you! I was here last night, and so was he. I'll swear to it in a court of law."

He would, too, even though he knew that if he ever set foot in a courtroom and revealed who he was, he would be arrested for his crimes and sent to prison at the very least, if not to the gallows. He couldn't let Pap be blamed for something he hadn't done, though.

Barstow gave a harsh laugh. "You think I give a hoot about a court of law? *I'm* the court of law around here, just like I always have been."

"Move aside, Matt," Pap grated. "This ain't your fight. They may kill me, but I'll take some o' the bastards to hell with me!"

One of the cowboys spoke up. "Somebody comin', Mr. Barstow!"

Barstow and the others looked around to see two riders galloping toward them from the direction of the settlement.

142

With a frown, the cattleman said, "One of 'em looks like Tom Reeder. Reckon he decided he better do like I told him, after all. Don't know who the other fella is."

Pap recognized the man with Reeder, though. "It's that hombre Parker who stopped by yesterday," he said.

Matt didn't know who Parker was and didn't care. All that mattered was that there would be two more witnesses on hand now, and maybe Barstow wouldn't carry out his threats in front of outsiders.

But then he realized that he was kidding himself. Barstow wouldn't be afraid of the marshal from Greenwood. Matt had already heard about how ineffective Reeder was, and anyway, the man didn't have any legal authority beyond the town limits. And during Parker's stop here at the soddy, he had seemed to be just a drifter.

"What do we do, boss?" one of the cowboys asked.

Before Barstow could reply, Reeder shouted, "Hold it! Hold it, you men!"

Barstow glared and said, "Reckon we better let him have his say. Not that it's gonna make a damned bit of difference."

They sat there on their horses as Reeder and Parker galloped up to the soddy and reined in. Matt got his first real look at Parker. The man was tall and muscular, with dark brown hair and sweeping longhorn mustaches. He wore range clothes and a flat-crowned, snuff-brown Stetson, and carried a Colt with well-worn walnut grips in a cross-draw rig. He might be just a drifter, but it was obvious he was a tough hombre.

"Mr. Barstow, just what is it you're plannin' to do here?" Marshal Reeder asked. He was pale and sweating, but he had some traces of gumption on his face and in his voice.

"I'm gonna do what I should've done a long time ago," Barstow rasped. "I'm gonna clean out this rat's nest of rustlers and killers. This whole valley's nothin' but a haven for outlaws."

"That's a dadblasted lie!" Pap spoke up. "The home-steaders who have filed claims here are honest, hard-workin' folks, every single one of 'em."

Barstow pointed again at the steers. "I told you in town I was right about them, Reeder, and there's the proof! We found these cows hidden close by here. I figure they were the old man's share from the bunch that was rustled last night. If we'd got here any later, they'd have already been butchered and the hides burned or buried!"

Matt looked straight at Reeder and Parker and said, "I don't know who stole those cows from the Boxed B, but Pap couldn't have had any part of it. He was right here in the soddy last night."

Barstow spat, making it clear what he thought of Matt's testimony.

Parker spoke up for the first time, saying in a hard voice, "What's that gal doing with a rope around her?"

"She took a shot at us when we rode up," Barstow said. "I told a couple of my boys to make sure she couldn't hurt anybody. These sodbusters already killed two of my hands last night, you know."

"I'm sorry if some o' your men got shot," Pap said, "but nobody from the valley had anything to do with it."

"You're wastin' your breath." Barstow turned his defiant gaze back to Reeder and Parker. "I'm gonna have every grown man in this valley tarred and feathered, and then them and their families have until the end of the day to get out. And they're gettin' off light, too. By rights, I ought to start stringin' 'em up one by one until they tell me exactly who killed my riders last night. Damn a country that don't have any trees tall enough to hang a rustler from, anyway."

Parker rested his hands on the horn and leaned forward in his saddle. "You're not going to tar and feather anybody, Barstow, and you're not going to run anybody off their claims, either," he said. "All you're going to do is get that damned lasso off that gal *right now*!"

144

Barstow drew in a deep breath and swelled up in anger, like a toad. His face looked like a thundercloud about to burst. "Who the hell says so?" he shouted.

The tall, tough-looking hombre looked straight back at him and said, "Uncle Sam, in the person o' me, Deputy United States Marshal Custis Long."

Chapter 17

Barstow was surprised by that revelation, as Longarm had figured he would be. The cattleman stared at him for a couple of seconds, unsure what to do next, but then resolve firmed up his rugged face again.

"You got no right to interfere," he barked. "This ain't a federal matter."

"The hell it ain't," Longarm shot right back at him. "It was the federal government that these homesteaders filed their claims with. The government has honored those claims, so that means it's my job to make sure *you* honor 'em, too, Barstow."

Barstow looked apoplectic, but he wasn't giving up. "I'm not runnin' 'em out because of the claims they filed. I'm runnin' 'em out because they're rustlers and owlhoots and murderin' skunks! And those are state crimes, not federal, damn it!"

Barstow was right about that. Although Longarm had the jurisdiction to go anywhere and do whatever was necessary to carry out his assignment, he wasn't supposed to interfere in local matters unless he was asked to do so by local authorities. Tom Reeder was the only one of those critters on hand, and Longarm wasn't sure the town marshal had the right to request that he intervene in this case.

All of which meant that if there was no way to do this legal and proper, Longarm would just have to do it illegal and improper. Either way, he wasn't going to allow Barstow to run roughshod over the settlers in this valley.

"These homesteaders are living on claims ceded to them by the federal government," Longarm argued. "That makes them the government's responsibility. That means I can't let you do what you're planning, Barstow."

The cattle baron snorted in disgust. "You can throw around as much fancy talk as you want, Long. Plain and simple fact o' the matter is, you're just one man. You can't stop me from doin' whatever I damn well please."

"Maybe not," Longarm said, "but I can damn well make sure you don't live to see it, old son."

Barstow's face darkened even more. "You're threatenin' me?"

"Nope. I'm just telling you that if you start the ball, you'll be the first one I kill." Longarm let his eyes flick to the other men just for a second. "But probably not the last."

One of the cowboys said, "Boss, I've heard about this fella. He's the one they call Longarm. Folks say he's rough as a cob and mighty slick with his gun."

Barstow jerked his head around. "Shut up! If you don't want to ride for the brand anymore, you can draw your pay and get the hell out of my sight!" He glowered at the other punchers. "The same goes for the rest of you!"

"Nobody said anything about drawin' our pay, boss," another man spoke up. "But if this fella really is a federal lawman, maybe we ought to listen to what he's got to say."

Longarm reached into his shirt pocket and drew out the leather folder that contained his badge and identification papers. Most of the time he kept it hidden in his saddlebags, but today he had it handy. He opened it and held it up so that all of them could see the sun glinting off the badge pinned inside the folder.

"That ought to take care of any questions about my bona fides," he said as he closed the folder and stowed it in his pocket again. "Now, I've got a few more things to say, and I'd advise you to listen, Barstow."

Barstow was still seething, but he grated, "Speak your piece."

Longarm nodded. "I ran into the Hell Riders last night. They were raiding a place a couple miles north of here."

"That'd be Harley Eggars's farm," Pap said. "Is ol' Harley all right?"

"I hope so, but I don't know for sure," Longarm told him. "I jumped the Hell Riders and drew them away from the place, but I didn't go back after I gave them the slip."

Barstow said, "That don't mean they didn't rustle my cows later."

"They could have," Longarm admitted again, "but the last time I saw them they were splitting up, like they were going to head back to Greenwood separately."

"Are they really monsters?" Pap asked.

Longarm had to smile. "Reckon that's open for debate," he said, "but I can tell you this much: their heads ain't really on fire." He reached into one of his saddlebags and brought out the hood he had found in Abilene's gear the night before. "This is what they wear."

Barstow shook his head in disbelief. "That's just some sort o' flour-sack hood."

"That's all it looks like now because it's broad daylight," Longarm explained. "But at night, this hood glows like it's on fire. When it flaps around in the wind, it looks like flames flickering. Put one of these on the head of an hombre who's galloping around and shooting at you, and you'd think his head was on fire, all right."

"So that's how they did it," Matt O'Hara said with interest. "I figured it had to be a trick of some kind."

149

"So did I," Claire put in. She had been released from the rope, and she stood to one side, rubbing one of her arms where the rough horsehide lasso had chafed it. "I knew nobody could ride around raising hell if his head was really on fire."

Glowering at Longarm, Barstow said, "Even if what you're sayin' is true, it don't prove a damned thing. Those sodbusters could still be the Hell Riders."

"Men from this valley have been shot and killed by those varmints," Pap said. "Good men, family men. You don't really think we'd kill our own just to make it easier to get back at you, do you, Barstow? Not even you can be that twisted by hate."

Barstow didn't answer. Longarm said, "There's plenty of evidence that the Hell Riders attacked the farmers here in the valley. What evidence do you have that they rustled your cattle and killed your men, Barstow? Did you see them with your own eyes?"

"I don't need to," Barstow said. "Three o' my boys told me all about it. They were out on the range last night when those damn Hell Riders hit the spread. They saw Teddy London and Boo Harper get gunned down."

"Is that the only time anybody's actually seen the Hell Riders on the Boxed B?" Longarm asked.

"Once is enough!"

"Those three witnesses . . . are they here today?"

"They sure are." Barstow waved a hand toward his riders. "Bud Miller, Dooley Thomas, and Ed Lawrence." He turned to look at them. "Come on up here, boys."

The three punchers eased their horses forward, but they seemed nervous and reluctant to do so. Longarm looked at them and said, "You saw the Hell Riders last night? You saw them rustle those cows and shoot down your pards?"

"That's right," one of the men replied. "Seen it with our own eyes, just like you said, mister."

"How many cattle went missing?"

"Between forty and fifty, I'd say."

Longarm pointed at the four steers. "Including those?"

"They must've been part of the bunch," the cowboy said. "You can see the Boxed B brand for yourself."

Barstow snorted and nodded in triumph.

Longarm ignored the cattleman and continued to concentrate on the three punchers. "Where did you find the steers?"

"They were in a gully over yonder, about a quarter of a mile, maybe half a mile from here." The spokesman for the trio of cowboys turned in his saddle to wave toward the north. "Somebody'd built a brush corral and penned them in it."

"Was it you three who found them?"

Miller, Thomas, and Lawrence didn't answer, but Barstow did. "What if it was them? What the hell does that have to do with anything?"

Longarm looked at Barstow and said, "Think about this. If Pap here was really a rustler, would he hide any stolen stock this close to his farm?"

"I told you, he planned to butcher those steers and burn or bury the hides!"

"Why didn't he go ahead and do that, then?" Longarm asked. He glanced at the sky. "The sun's been up for hours. Plenty of time to get started on dirty work like that. Maybe even finish it. But instead, those critters are still alive and healthy." The big lawman switched his gaze to Pap. "How'd you spend your morning, Pap?"

"Workin' in the crops, like I always do," Pap replied. "I didn't know a durned thing about any stolen cows."

Bud Miller pointed at Pap and said, "What do you expect the old bastard to say? He's lyin' to save his own skin!"

Matt O'Hara spoke up. "Pap's telling the truth. He was here all night, and he's been working in the field this morning. He couldn't have rustled any cattle."

Barstow still glared, but a frown was beginning to form on his face, too. Whether he wanted to believe it or not, what Longarm and the others were saying made sense.

Longarm nodded toward the three punchers and said, "I'll bet these ol' boys didn't have any trouble finding those steers, did they? Pretty much went right to them?"

"No," Barstow snapped. "We had to look around a little while before they found them."

"A little while," Longarm repeated. "Just long enough to make it look good."

One of the cowboys burst out, "Damn it, he's twistin' everything around, Mr. Barstow! It wasn't that way. You know me and Bud and Ed wouldn't ever steal from you!"

Bud Miller said, "Shut up, Dooley. The boss ain't gonna believe this lawman's lies."

"What reason do I have to lie?" Longarm asked.

"To protect these damn sodbusters!"

Longarm looked at Barstow. "Think about it," he said. "Think about it mighty hard. The Hell Riders show up a month or so ago and start raiding the farms here in the valley. Not long after that, your cattle start to disappear. The Hell Riders must be to blame, right? And you hate these homesteaders so much, you decide *they* must be the Hell Riders, even though that doesn't make any sense. Like Pap said, they wouldn't raid their own farms just to get back at you."

"How do we know any of that really happened?" Barstow demanded. "How do we know all those stories about the Hell Riders raidin' their farms weren't a pack of lies?"

"I can show you the graves of the men who were killed by them demons," Pap said in a quiet, solemn voice. "I can show you the crops that were trampled and the soddies that were knocked down. Those graves and those ruined farms, there's your proof, Barstow."

Marshal Reed spoke up at last. "They're telling the

truth, Mr. Barstow. I know it, and you know it, too. You just don't want to admit it."

Barstow glared at the local star packer. "Don't you go tellin' me what I know and don't know, Reeder. Remember, I can get the town council to fire you any time I want!"

Despite being gray-faced, Reeder lifted his chin and said, "You go right ahead if that's what you want, Mr. Barstow, but it won't change the truth any."

The marshal of Greenwood had more guts than Longarm had given him credit for.

Pressing on, Longarm said, "Those fellas who were killed last night, London and Harper, were they particular pards of Miller, Thomas, and Lawrence here?"

"Hell, I don't know," Barstow said.

But several of the other cowboys had begun to look askance at the trio who had found the steers hidden in the gully and claimed to have seen the Hell Riders the night before. One of the punchers said, "Yeah, that's true, Marshal. The five of 'em hired on together a year or so ago, and they pretty much stayed to themselves after that. Never did have much to do with anybody else."

"So it could be they decided to take advantage of the trouble the Hell Riders were causing in these parts and start rustling Boxed B stock," Longarm said. "Then there was a falling-out amongst thieves for some reason, and London and Harper wound up dead. Who better to blame for that than the Hell Riders? And just to make sure everybody made the connection between the Hell Riders and the homesteaders here in the valley, they hid some of the stolen stock close by last night and pretended to find it this morning."

"That's crazy and you can't prove a lick of it," Bud Miller said.

Longarm smiled. "I'll bet I can, old son. I'll bet if I poke around for a while, I'll find out where you've been selling those cows you widelooped, and I'll even dig up somebody willing to testify it was you boys he bought 'em from. Might even find where you cached all the loot you've made from this operation." He looked at the cattle baron. "You agree to leave these homesteaders alone, Barstow, and I'll bring you all the proof you'll need to see that I'm right. Then the whole thing can be handled the right way." He turned his gaze back to Miller, Thomas, and Lawrence. "No tar and feathers. Just a gallows at the county seat."

"Damn it, you won't hang me!" Dooley Thomas cried as his hand stabbed toward the gun on his hip. "It was all Bud's idea!"

Miller and Lawrence slapped leather, too. Now that Thomas's nerve had broken and he had implicated them all, they had no choice but to try to shoot their way out of here.

Longarm expected that, had been trying to prod them into it, in fact, knowing that he might *not* be able to find enough proof to convince Barstow. His hand flashed across his body, palmed the Colt from the cross-draw rig, and brought the revolver up with blinding speed. Flame spurted from the muzzle as he fired.

Longarm's instincts had told him that Miller was the most dangerous of the trio, so he went for him first. Miller rocked back in the saddle, and the gun in his hand went off as Longarm's bullet slammed into his chest. The rustler's shot went wide, and Miller, toppling backward off his horse, didn't get another one off.

Pap's rifle blasted before Longarm could pull the trigger a second time. Thomas slewed sideways and dropped his gun as the slug shattered his right shoulder. He clutched at it, whimpering in pain, and slumped forward over his horse's neck.

That left Lawrence, and even though he had his gun in his hand, he didn't try to fire. Instead, he yanked his horse around and dug in the spurs, sending the animal leaping toward Claire. She was too shocked to move, and even as Longarm fired at Lawrence and missed, he saw that the man intended to grab Claire and use her as a hostage to get away. Longarm's finger eased off the trigger. Lawrence was already too close to Claire to risk another shot.

But then Matt O'Hara leaped into the air, tackling Lawrence just as the rustler was reaching for Claire. The collision jolted both men. Matt was knocked backward, but he managed to hang on to Lawrence's shirt and haul the man off the horse. They crashed to the ground together.

Longarm jumped off his horse and ran toward the men. His gun was in his hand, but he still couldn't chance a shot. Lawrence's gun had been knocked out of his hand when he landed, but he was putting up a desperate fight anyway, flailing away at Matt. The young man seemed to have forgotten about his wound as he slugged back at the rustler. They rolled over and over as they grappled and punched.

Matt landed a hard right that sent Lawrence sprawling on his back. Matt lunged and came down on top of him, driving a knee into Lawrence's belly. He kept the rustler pinned there and smashed a right, a left, and another right into his face. The blows jerked Lawrence's head from side to side.

Longarm leaned down, got an arm around Matt, and pulled him up and off the stunned rustler. Lawrence's face was covered with blood. His nose was smashed flat and both eyes were swelling shut. All the fight had been knocked out of him.

"Take it easy," Longarm told Matt as the young man struggled to get out of his grasp. "This fracas is over, and the gal's safe."

"Claire?" Matt gasped. He twisted his head around to look for her. "Claire, are you all right?"

She appeared in front of him as Longarm let him go. "I'm fine," she told him. "That varmint never even laid a hand on me."

155

"Thank God," Matt said. He threw his arms around her. "Thank God you're not hurt."

Then his eyes rolled up in his head and he sagged against her as his knees folded up, so that she had to hang on to him to keep him from falling. "Oh, hell!" she said. "You're bleeding all over again. How many times am I gonna have to clean you up, you damn loco fool?"

Her voice was gentle as she said it, though, and Longarm had to chuckle as he holstered his Colt and bent down to grab Ed Lawrence and haul the rustler to his feet. He didn't know the whole story here, but he would have been willing to bet it wouldn't be long before Pap had himself a brand-new grandson-in-law to help him work this homestead.

Chapter 18

Bud Miller was dead, but Dooley Thomas and Ed Lawrence were both alive and eager to talk. Thomas wouldn't shut up, in fact, as Longarm did a rough job of patching up his wounded shoulder.

"It was all Bud's idea," Thomas said again through teeth gritted against the pain. "He's the one who said we ought to rustle them cows and blame it on the Hell Riders. Then when Boo and Teddy went to squabblin' with him about how we've been divvyin' up the dinero, it was Bud who shot 'em. Ed and me didn't like it. No, sir, not one bit."

Of course, it was mighty convenient that the mastermind behind the rustling just happened to be the hombre who was dead and couldn't deny the charges, Longarm thought, but he didn't really care whether Thomas was telling the whole truth. Both of the surviving rustlers would wind up behind bars where they belonged, and while Barstow would no doubt continue to make life miserable for the homesteaders in the valley, at least he wouldn't have the excuse of believing them to be the Hell Riders anymore.

When Longarm was through patching up Thomas, Reeder said, "I'll take charge of the prisoners, Marshal.

They can stay locked up in my jail until the sheriff can send some deputies over to fetch them to the county seat for trial."

Longarm nodded. "Sounds good to me. I know you'll take good care of 'em and not let anybody take the law into their own hands." He gave Barstow a meaningful look as he added that last part.

Barstow was still angry—that seemed to be his natural state—but he was also shaken by the discovery that some of his own men had been rustling his cattle. He said, "Don't worry, Long. I've washed my hands o' this whole mess."

"And you're going to leave the homesteaders alone?"

"They still don't have any right to be here, to my way o' thinkin'," the cattle baron growled. "But . . . if they don't interfere with me, I'll steer clear o' them."

Pap said, "We never wanted anything 'cept to be left alone to work our farms, Barstow."

"Fine," Barstow snapped. The two old men gave each other curt nods.

Longarm didn't figure the truce would hold forever, but maybe it would last for a while.

He stepped into the soddy and looked at the bunk where Claire was wrapping fresh bandages around Matt O'Hara's torso after cleaning up the blood that had welled from the wound in his side. "We ain't been introduced," he said. "Name's Custis Long."

"Matt O'Hara," the young man said, wincing a little as Claire pulled the bandages tight.

"You were in here the other day when I stopped by, weren't you?"

"Yeah," O'Hara admitted.

"Any particular reason you didn't want anybody to know that?"

The young fella had sand; he had demonstrated that by the way he had jumped Lawrence to save Claire, even though he was unarmed and injured. But Longarm didn't like unanswered questions, and he sensed there were some big ones surrounding Matt O'Hara.

"No, no reason," O'Hara said, but he turned his head as he spoke so that he wouldn't have to look into Longarm's eyes.

"Wouldn't happen to be because you're on the run from the law, would it?"

"Why don't you just leave him alone?" Claire snapped. "Can't you see that he's hurt?"

"I can see that," Longarm said. "I'm just wondering how he got that bullet hole in his side."

She stood up and faced him, with a look in her eyes as fierce as that of a mama bear protecting her cubs. "I can tell you that. He got hurt helping us fight off the Hell Riders a few nights ago. And he won't let it heal up because he keeps getting into scrapes to help me and Pap."

"Got a good look at the Hell Riders, did you?" Longarm asked O'Hara, looking over Claire's shoulder as he did so.

Matt didn't seem to mind talking about that. He nodded and said, "Yeah. I even plugged one of them."

"We've got that in common, then, because I killed one of them last night. That's where I got that hood I showed everybody outside."

"I knew it had to be a damn trick," Claire said. She frowned. "But if they aren't Barstow's men, then who in blazes are they?"

"I'm working on that," Longarm told her. "I even know who some of them are. The more important question is who are they working for?"

Claire shook her head. "I don't have any earthly idea. As far as I know, Barstow's the only one in these parts with any sort of grudge against us homesteaders."

"Well, I'll keep thinking on it," Longarm promised. "I guess I'll be riding on." He looked at Matt O'Hara again. "That is, if you're sure there's nothing else you want to tell me about."

"Nothing to tell," Claire said, shooing Longarm toward the door. "Thank you for everything you've done, Marshal, but we'll be fine now."

Longarm made an effort not to grin and gave her a solemn nod instead. "All right. Be seeing you, miss." He tugged on the brim of his Stetson and then walked out of the soddy.

Matt O'Hara was hiding something, no doubt about that. Probably a criminal past. Longarm might look into that, or he might not. He hadn't decided yet. But either way it would have to wait. He still had more pressing matters to clear up.

Namely, Dog McCluskey, the rest of the Hell Riders, and their mysterious boss.

"He didn't believe me," Matt said when Longarm was gone. "He knows I'm an outlaw."

"He doesn't know anything of the sort," Claire insisted. She perched on the edge of the bunk and took his hand. "He may suspect, but he doesn't know. And he won't, if me and Pap have anything to say about it."

"You're being sort of quick to make promises for what Pap'll do, aren't you?"

She blew her breath out. "Shoot, you just leave Pap to me. I've had that old man wrapped around my little finger since I was big enough to toddle around and suck my thumb."

Somehow, Matt didn't doubt that.

"I thought you were mad at me because I'm an owl-hoot." He knew it might be unwise to bring up that subject, but he didn't want things left unsaid between them. He hadn't known about the problems that existed between him and Abigail Phelps until it was too late to do anything about them. He didn't want that to happen again.

"Well . . . you're a funny kind of owlhoot. All you've done since you got here is try to help us. You won't find

160

many outlaws who care more about other folks than they do about themselves."

He was relieved to hear her say that, but he kept his face expressionless as he said, "There's no getting around the fact that I tried to rob that bank and shot poor Harvey Lapreste."

Claire frowned. "Maybe not, but you've tried to tell us your reasons. We didn't want to listen. Maybe now we ought to."

"Is this because that rustler tried to grab you as a hostage and I stopped him?"

"Well, can you think of a better reason than saving somebody's life?" Claire sighed and shook her head. "I swear, Matt O'Hara, you are one stubborn and prideful son of a bitch. You done a good thing. I'm grateful to you. Pap's grateful to you. Can't you just accept that and maybe take advantage of the situation?"

"I'm not one to take advantage," Matt said.

"I'll say! Why, I bet if I took all my clothes off right now and crawled into that bunk with you, you wouldn't even try to do anything about it."

"I just lost a lot of blood, remember? I'm not sure I *could* do anything about it."

He couldn't get the image of Claire with all her clothes off out of his head, though.

She stood up and reached for the top button of her shirt. "Why don't we just see about that?"

He struggled to sit up. "Claire, damn it, no! Have you gone loco? Pap's right outside, and so are a bunch of other folks!"

To his utter shock, she started to cry. She had only unfastened one button, and she left off there. Instead, she dropped to her knees beside the bed and rested her head on his chest as his strength deserted him and he sagged back on the mattress and pillow.

"Damn it, Matt," she whispered as tears rolled down her

161

cheeks, "haven't you figured out yet that I love you, owl-hoot or no owlhoot?"

Love . . . Now that he thought about it, he couldn't recollect Abigail ever saying that she loved him, even though they had kept company for months and been engaged. She had talked about their wedding, and what their life would be like after they were married, but as for saying that she loved him . . . Nope, not once.

But Claire, who had known him for less than three full days and been mad at him pretty much the whole time . . . *she* loved him.

The crazy thing was, he felt the same way about her.

He gave her a weak pat on the back with his right hand and swallowed hard before he managed to get out the words. "I . . . I love you, too."

That was where things stood when Pap cleared his throat in the doorway. Matt looked up to see the old-timer glaring at them. Pap just stood there for a second; then sighed and shook his head.

"I knowed it," he said. "I seen it in her eyes. Might as well try to stop a rock from rollin' downhill or a river from flowin' downstream. You just thought you had trouble before, young fella. You're in for a whole heap of it now, you know that, don't you?"

"Yeah," Matt said. "I know."

But somehow he couldn't stop himself from grinning as he said it.

Longarm asked Marshal Tom Reeder to keep quiet about him being a lawman for the time being.

"Sure, Marshal," Reeder said with a nod. He had the two prisoners loaded onto their horses and was ready to start back to Greenwood with them. "I'll keep it under my hat. You can count on me."

"Much obliged. I've still got to round up Dog McCluskey, and I don't want him knowing that he's got a star packer hot on his trail. He's liable to cut and run if he finds out."

"Well, he won't find out from me," Reeder promised, "and I'll have a talk with Mr. Barstow and his men and tell them to keep quiet about it, too."

Longarm nodded his thanks. He mounted up, ticked a finger against the brim of his hat in farewell, and rode off, angling south instead of east toward Greenwood. He wanted to take a better look at the rest of the valley, to see if the theory he had put together in his mind was going to hold together.

He spent the rest of the morning and most of the afternoon ranging up and down the valley, keeping his eyes on the ground much of the time. In numerous places, he found the signs he was looking for, although it appeared that someone had tried to cover up some of them. He dismounted and inspected a few of them at close range to be sure of what he was looking at.

Satisfied that his suppositions were right, he rode on, heading more toward Greenwood now. He was turning over plans in his head, trying to decide on the right course of action, when he spotted the wagon rolling over the prairie ahead of him. A smile touched his wide mouth as he recognized the vehicle.

It didn't take long for him to catch up to it. As he drew alongside, he called, "Howdy, folks."

Roy Archer hauled back on the reins, bringing the team to a halt. "Mr. Parker!" he greeted Longarm. "Good day to you, sir."

"Hello, Custis," Guinevere greeted him from her place on the seat beside her brother.

Longarm leaned on the saddlehorn. "Still looking for butterflies, I see."

"It's a never-ending search," Archer said as he returned Longarm's grin. "Are you seeking something in particular, or simply riding around and enjoying this beautiful day?"

"Actually, I *was* looking for something. I was thinking

about staking a claim here in the valley myself, if I can find some good land that's not already being homesteaded."

"You're going to be a farmer?" Guinevere said. She sounded like she couldn't believe that.

"I figure it's time for me to settle down," Longarm said. "A man can't drift his whole life. He needs to try to make something of himself."

"Well, that's an admirable goal," Archer said, "but I think you can find a better place to do it than this. Haven't you noticed that the crops being raised here aren't of the best quality?"

"Well, they do seem a mite sparse in places," Longarm admitted. "Countryside seems to be plagued with prairie dogs, too. Little varmints have dug their holes everywhere."

"Indeed. Plus, there's all the talk in town about trouble between the homesteaders and the cattle ranchers around here, especially one named Barstow." Archer gave a solemn shake of his head. "I'm afraid I wouldn't want to claim any land in this valley. I think most of the home-steaders will be forced to abandon their farms before too much longer."

"You could be right," Longarm said with a sage nod. "Maybe I ought to look elsewhere for a place to settle down."

"I think that would be wise." Archer perked up. "But since you're here, why don't you accompany us the rest of the day? Guinevere and I both enjoy your company. Don't we, Guin?"

"We certainly do," she agreed, and Longarm saw the sparkle in her eyes as she spoke. She was remembering all the times they had made love, he thought. To be honest, those times were sort of weighing on his mind, too.

"Sure, I'll ride with you," he said. "Maybe you can teach me how to catch butterflies."

"Oh, that's something that takes a long time to learn," Archer said as he flapped the reins and got the horses moving again. "But you're welcome to observe. If, of course, we come across any suitable specimens. You can't tell when that will happen. Sometimes our efforts go for naught."

Longarm heeled his horse into motion and walked the animal alongside the wagon. "I know the feeling."

Archer kept up his usual animated chatter as they moved at a slow, deliberate pace across the valley. Longarm's mind was only half on what the lepidopterist was saying. He was thinking about everything he had discovered over the past couple of days, as well as trading the occasional meaningful glance with Guinevere Archer.

Suddenly, Archer hauled back on the reins and said, "There! Did you see it?" Excitement gripped him.

"What was it, Roy?" his sister asked.

"I think it was a red admiral." He scrambled down from the seat. "*Vanessa atalanta*. It was there on top of that hill."

He pointed to a slight rise as he hurried to the back of the wagon and opened the door. Snatching a long-handled net from inside, he trotted off in the direction he had indicated. "I have to see if I can catch it!" he called over his shoulder. "I'll be back!"

"But not for a while, I daresay," Guinevere said with a laugh. "He'll probably spot a dozen more specimens along the way and try to catch them, too."

Longarm had reined in beside the wagon. "Are you saying he's going to be gone for a while?"

"That's exactly what I'm saying." Her tongue darted out and licked over her lips. "You've seen the rear of this wagon, Custis. You know there's a considerable amount of room back there. We could put it to good use."

Longarm frowned. "I don't know. It sounds mighty interesting, but with your brother running around out there, so close by . . ."

"Don't worry about Roy. As I told you, he'll be gone for a good while." She gave a defiant toss of her head that made her blond hair swirl around her shoulders. "Anyway,

I live my own life and make my own decisions. My brother may cling to some archaic notion that he's in charge of me simply because I'm a female, but I assure you, that's not the case."

Longarm made up his mind and nodded. "All right. You've convinced me."

Guinevere stood up and extended a hand toward him. "Help me down." As Longarm closed his fingers around her warm, soft hand, she added, "I promise you, Custis, you're not going to regret this."

Longarm wasn't so sure about that, but as he saw the look in her eyes, he knew there was no turning back now.

Chapter 19

"Sit down there," Guinevere said, pointing to a padded bench in the back of the wagon. She had left the door open a few inches so that some of the late-afternoon sunlight could enter the vehicle, along with fresh air to dilute the acrid smell of the chemicals Archer used in his butterfly collecting. Also, they would be more likely to hear Guinevere's brother if he came back to the wagon.

Longarm sat down and watched as Guinevere hiked up her skirts and reached underneath them to adjust her undergarments. Her legs looked good, long and sleek in cotton stockings that ended just above her knees. The white flash of her thighs was enticing as she got ready for him.

"Take your gun off and pull your trousers down," she said as she came closer to him, close enough so that he smelled the faint musky scent of her arousal.

"This'll do," Longarm said as he unbuttoned his denim trousers and freed his stiffening shaft from the tight confines of his long underwear.

"Well, all right," Guinevere said. "I wish we could be naked together, like we were before, but I suppose this is more discreet. And exciting in its own way. Both of us being nearly fully dressed, I mean."

She turned so that she faced away from him and pulled her skirts up higher, revealing the bare, rounded cheeks of her bottom. Straddling his legs, she lowered herself onto him. The tip of his shaft found the already moist portal between her legs. With a sigh of pleasure, she sank down onto it, letting it penetrate her one slow, delicious inch at a time.

Longarm reached around her to close his hands over her breasts and caress them through her clothing. She tipped her head back. Strands of her blond hair tickled his face. She gasped as the head of his shaft hit bottom. He had filled her completely.

"Custis," she whispered. "Oh, my God. Custis . . ."

Neither of them moved for a long moment as they both sat there savoring the sensations that surged through them. Then Guinevere began a slow thrusting of her hips. Seated on the narrow bench with his back against the side wall of the wagon, Longarm couldn't move, but he didn't have to. Guinevere continued to pump her hips, panting with each thrust.

Her pace increased, and as it did, Longarm felt his arousal growing. He knew he couldn't hold out for very long under this exquisite torture. He slid his hands down her body, reached under her skirts, and pressed his fingers against the soft curves of her bare hips. He drove upward as much as he could, drilling the spike of his manhood into her.

"Yes, yes!" she said as she leaned forward a little and rested her hands on her knees. That gave her leverage to buck against him even harder. Her inner muscles clamped tightly on him, as if she were trying to milk his climax from him.

It worked. Like a volcano, his shaft erupted, his seed spilling from him in spurt after white-hot spurt. Shudders of culmination rippled through Guinevere's body as she quivered in Longarm's embrace. A long, drawn-out "Ahh-hhh!" of satisfaction came from her lips. Longarm groaned as he clamped his fingers on her thighs and emptied himself inside her.

Guinevere leaned back against him with her head on his shoulder. "You see?" she murmured. "I told you there would be plenty of time."

"Reckon you were right about that," Longarm told her.

She lingered there on his lap for a moment, then as he softened and slipped out of her, she stood up and turned to face him.

When she did, there was a gun in her hand.

It was only a little two-shot derringer, very similar to the one that Longarm sometimes carried, but at this range even a small-caliber slug would make a mighty big mess of his brain. Longarm let his eyes widen in surprise, even though he wasn't really all that shocked, and said, "What the hell! I thought I was doing what you wanted—"

"You can drop the act, Custis," she said, her voice cold and hard as ice. "You may have fooled my brother, but I wasn't taken in by your lies. Who are you? A Pinkerton? A deputy sheriff?"

"Try a deputy U.S. marshal," he said, letting his own voice harden to match hers. He hadn't been sure they were taken in by his pose of ignorance, but he had been hoping they were. He'd wanted some more time to figure out the best way to handle the situation.

It was obvious now, though, that he wasn't going to get that time. He would have to turn the tables on Guinevere somehow, arrest her and her brother, and then deal with the Hell Riders later.

"No, thanks," she said with a cool smile. "I've already tried a deputy U.S. marshal. Several times, in fact. And I have to admit you were quite good, Custis. I'm sorry that you have to die."

"It doesn't have to be that way. I can ride on and forget about what I've found here in the valley. Hell, just give me Dog McCluskey. He's the only one I'm really after. I didn't even know the Hell Riders existed until a couple of days ago."

"You make it sound tempting," Guinevere admitted. "But I'm afraid that even though we've been acquainted for only a short time, I already know you too well, Custis. All the investigating you've done tells me that you'd never let this go. Why, it was probably you who killed poor Abilene last night, wasn't it? I knew you'd slipped out of the hotel room, and when Roy told me someone had interfered with the raid on that farm, I suspected it must have been you."

"You didn't sleep through me leaving after all, then?"

"No, of course not. But I was hoping that you'd simply gone to have a drink or gamble in one of the saloons, not that you were sticking your nose in our business."

"Some business," Longarm said. "Driving a bunch of homesteaders off their claims and killing the ones who don't want to go, all the while blaming the whole mess on Barstow."

"Mr. Barstow is a harsh, unpleasant man. He made a very convenient scapegoat. Roy and I figured that out very soon after we arrived in Greenwood, just by listening to the conversations among the townspeople."

"Yeah, I reckon you've pulled schemes like this before, haven't you? Did you come up with the idea for the Hell Riders before or after you discovered the salt deposits?"

Guinevere laughed. "If you've got so much of it figured out already, Custis, why don't you tell me?"

"All right, I will," he said. The derringer in her hand had been rock-steady so far, but he didn't figure it would hurt anything to stall for time. "First of all, it wasn't butterflies that brought you and your brother here. I reckon he likes to catch 'em and collect 'em, all right, but that's not what you were really after. That was just an excuse for you to drive around and search for mineral deposits."

"How in the world do you know that?" she asked.

Longarm shrugged. "That contraption that fell out of

170

the case in front of the hotel in Greenwood wasn't a butterfly net. It was the casing for an auger that he uses to bore down into the ground and take samples from below the surface. Those flasks probably hold the chemicals that he uses to test the samples. Maybe even the ones that made those hoods glow like fire when the Hell Riders wore them."

Guinevere sighed. "Yes, I was afraid you weren't as unintelligent as you were acting. Go on."

"Mind if I light up a cheroot?"

"I suppose it won't do any harm. Be very careful about it, though. I don't have to indulge you. I could just pull the triggers right now and be done with this."

Longarm took a cheroot from his pocket and continued. "I knew somebody had been boring holes in the ground around here, because I saw them scattered across the valley. Took 'em for prairie dog holes at first, until I studied 'em a mite closer. Today I found more holes that had been covered up, so I knew somebody was trying to hide something. Found some places where the salt formations come right up to the surface, too. I was already thinking there must be a high concentration of salt in the ground around here because the crops grew so poorly. Those sodbusters really would be better off moving on. They'll never make a go of it around here." He put the cheroot in his mouth and clamped his teeth on it. "You and your brother weren't patient enough to wait for them to discover that on their own, though. You wanted to run 'em off now." He took out a match, his motions still slow and deliberate so that he wouldn't spook Guinevere into pulling the triggers of that derringer. "I'll bet Barstow planned to file on the valley once the homesteaders were gone. He'd have been surprised to find out that your partners back in Washington had already gobbled up all the claims."

"How do you know we have partners?"

"You have to have somebody close to the government land office, maybe even working there, so you can grab the claims you want before anybody else has a chance to file on them. Like I said, I reckon you've worked this scheme before and have it down pat."

"All over the country, in fact," she said with pride in her voice. "And in Mexico and South America, too. The various mineral deposits we've found have made us rich . . . but not rich enough."

Longarm snapped the lucifer into life with his thumbnail and held the flame to the tip of the cheroot. He puffed on the gasper and got it going. "Some folks can never be rich enough," he said around the cheroot.

"I think we're done here," Guinevere said as she backed off toward the workbench on the other side of the wagon. "Roy will be back soon, and he can figure out some way to dispose of your body."

Longarm came to his feet and shook his head. "You don't want to shoot me," he said. "The killings that the Hell Riders have done are their fault, not yours."

"I'm sure a court wouldn't see it that way, since they were working for us." The hand holding the derringer came up. "No, Custis, I'm sorry, but this is the way it has to be."

"I'm sorry, too," Longarm said, and meant it.

Then he tossed the still-burning lucifer past her, onto the table right behind her.

Guinevere cried out in alarm and started to turn, saying, "Good Lord! The acetate—"

Longarm knew the smell in the air came from the chemical Archer used to kill the butterflies he captured. The stuff was highly flammable, and Guinevere would know that, too. Her instinctive reaction in not wanting a burning match to get anywhere near the stuff made her pull the derringer out of line, and Longarm moved like a striking snake, swatting the little gun aside and sending it flying across the wagon.

He hit Guinevere in the jaw, pulling his punch so that he only stunned her rather than doing any real damage. Then

172

as he put his left arm around her to keep her from collapsing, he used his right hand to snuff out the lucifer where it lay on the table.

Guinevere hung loosely in the circle of his arm, only half-conscious as he took her to the rear of the wagon and pushed the door open with his foot. Before he could go down the steps with her, he heard the sound of a gun being cocked.

"Put her down and step out here, Mr. Parker," Roy Archer said as he glared at Longarm over the barrel of a Colt .45.

"Be careful of that hogleg, old son," Longarm said. "You go to shooting and you might hit your sister."

"What have you done to her?" Archer demanded.

"She ain't hurt. She just hit her head—"

Guinevere let out a moan and started to struggle in Longarm's grip as her senses returned to her. "Don't believe him, Roy!" she cried out. "He's a lawman! He knows about the salt and the Hell Riders!"

Longarm would have walloped her again, but it wouldn't do any good now. She had already warned her brother about him. But she could still come in handy. Longarm tightened his grip on her and kept her between him and Archer. It bothered him to use a woman as a shield, but it would bother him even more to let this pair of schemers and killers get away. He started to reach across his body for his gun.

"Well, this is a shame," Archer said. Then he pulled the trigger.

Guinevere opened her mouth to scream, but no sound came out before the bullet smashed into her, driving her back against Longarm. He felt a line of fire rake across his side as the slug went all the way through her and creased him as it burst out of her body. The shot would have killed them both if the bullet hadn't been deflected somewhat by one of Guinevere's ribs.

173

Longarm felt himself falling backward, knocked off his feet by the woman's deadweight slamming against him. He got his hand on his gun and drew it as he toppled off his feet. Another slug went past his ear, so close that he felt as much as heard the wind-rip of its passage. Landing awkwardly, he thrust the Colt under Guinevere's arm and triggered twice.

Archer spun around as the bullets ripped into him. He staggered a few steps, twisted back toward Longarm, and fired again. The bullet knocked splinters from the jamb of the wagon door. Longarm shoved Guinevere's body aside and lunged forward, rolling down the steps. He came to a stop on his belly and tilted his gun up to fire again just as flame gouted from the muzzle of Archer's weapon.

Archer's bullet whined over Longarm's head, but the slug from the big lawman's gun smashed into Archer's midsection, doubling him over. Archer's Colt slipped from his fingers and thudded to the ground as he struggled to stay on his feet. He failed, pitching forward to lie in a crumpled heap on the ground.

Longarm scrambled up. His side hurt where Archer's first shot had nicked him, but he could tell it wasn't bleeding much. He looked down at Guinevere where she lay just inside the wagon, and even in the rapidly fading light of dusk, he could see that her eyes held no life. Her own brother had killed her.

Longarm stalked over to Archer and hooked a boot toe under his shoulder to roll him onto his back. The front of the man's shirt was soaked with blood from the three wounds, but he was still breathing. His chest rose and fell in a ragged rhythm. His eyes fluttered open, reminding Longarm of those butterflies the man chased.

"P-Parker?"

"The name's Custis Long," Longarm told him. "Deputy U.S. marshal."

"Then . . . Guin was right . . . about you . . . you weren't to be . . . trusted. . . . Poor girl."

Longarm felt like emptying the rest of the bullets in his gun into the bastard's face, but instead he said, "You killed her, you know."

"Like I said . . . a shame." Archer's face twisted in agony. When the spasm passed, he said, "How . . . how did you know?"

"You ain't going to live long enough for me to explain all of it," Longarm said in a hard voice. "Not gutshot like that. But I found the holes you bored and recognized that apparatus of yours for what it really is. I found one of the horses from your wagon team in the corral last night, too, sweaty from having been ridden. You had your sister keep me occupied while you rode out to meet with Abilene, McCluskey, and the rest of the Hell Riders and give them their marching orders for the night."

Archer laughed. Thickened by blood, it was a ghastly sound. "They have their . . . orders for tonight too . . . they're going to . . . clean those homesteaders out of the valley . . . once and for all."

Longarm felt a chill go through him at those words.

"Tomorrow the valley . . . and all the salt underneath it . . . will belong to us," Archer said, and he sounded for all the world like he thought he had won. He chuckled— and the chuckle turned into a grotesque rattle in his throat as he died.

Longarm reloaded his gun, his brain working as swiftly as his hands did. Archer had turned the Hell Riders loose on the settlers in the valley. By morning, a lot of them might be dead, including Claire and Pap.

Unless Longarm could stop them, and he knew that one man was no match for the whole gang. He had to find some help from somewhere. . . .

And as a plan began to form in his head, he turned and ran back to the wagon, darting inside and remaining for several minutes before he came out, grabbed his horse, and galloped off into the gathering darkness.

Chapter 20

"I never seen that gal quite so happy," Pap confided in Matt O'Hara as they sat and watched Claire washing up the dishes after supper. She sang to herself under her breath. "I don't mind tellin' you, son, it scares me a mite. I sorta wish she'd go back to cussin' and yellin' like she usually does."

"Give her time," Matt said with a smile. "I'm sure she'll get back to normal."

"I ain't so sure about that," Pap said. "I got a feelin' things ain't ever gonna be normal around here again. O' course, that ain't necessarily a *bad* thing, mind you."

Claire glanced over her shoulder at them. Pap sat on the stool next to the bunk where Matt lay. "You two quit whispering amongst yourselves," she told them. "You'll make me think you're plotting against me."

"Why, we wouldn't never do that, darlin'," Pap protested. "Matt an' me, we was just talkin'—"

"Mighty friendly now, aren't you? You were worried about him being an owlhoot, remember?"

"No more'n you were, gal. Anyway, I reckon sometimes things happen that folks don't really have no control over—"

Claire's head came up. "Listen! What's that?"

Matt heard it, too. It was like thunder rolling across the prairie, or the sound of distant drums. Hoofbeats. A lot of them.

And he knew that couldn't be anything good.

Claire jerked her hands from the dishpan and whirled to the rifle that was leaning against the wall. She grabbed the weapon without bothering to dry her hands. Pap sprang to his feet, his own rifle gripped in his gnarled hands. He blew out the lamp as Claire flung the door open.

"It's the Hell Riders!" she cried. "I see those damn burning heads!"

They all knew now how the trick was worked, but knowing that didn't make the sight of the raiders swooping down on the farm any less terrifying. More than a score of killers thundered through the night toward the soddy. Colt flame bloomed in the darkness as the Hell Riders opened fire.

"Get down, gal!" Pap shouted as he lunged at Claire and looped an arm around her. With a sound like that of bees buzzing, bullets came through the open doorway. Pap grunted in pain as he bore Claire to the floor.

"Pap!" she screamed. "You're hit!"

"Just . . . a scratch," he grated. "Get that . . . door shut!"

Matt rolled off the bunk and hit the hard-packed dirt floor on hands and knees. He crawled toward the door and got hold of it, swinging the wooden panel shut as more bullets whipped through the air less than a foot above his head. The slugs began to hit the door with heavy thuds. The door was thick enough to stop the bullets for the time being, but as much lead as the Hell Riders were pouring at the soddy, it might not hold up for long.

"Where's my pistol?" Matt asked above the racket.

"Damn it, you're hurt!" Claire said. "You can't be fighting again!"

He moved toward the sound of her voice, reached out, found her arm, and closed his hand around it. "None of us

178

have any choice," he told her. "Those kill-crazy bastards will wipe us all out if we don't stop them."

But three people against so many ruthless outlaws wouldn't stand a chance. This was no hit-and-run raid, Matt sensed. The Hell Riders had come to make sure that everyone who opposed them died.

"Here you go, son," Pap said. Matt reached out with his other hand and found the butt of his Colt as the old-timer held it out to him. "Reckon we'll hold out as long as we can and take as many o' them with us as we can, too!"

"Matt . . ." Claire snuggled against him, her trembling body warm in the darkness. "Oh, Matt, we could've had a life together."

"We've got what we have," he told her as he pressed his face into her thick brown hair. "That's more than some people."

And it was more than he ever would have had with Abigail Phelps, he realized. Even though it might be cut short, the time he had spent with Claire meant more to him than anything else in his life. More than his ranch, more than the broken engagement, more than the stupid attempt at bank robbery that had put him on the run from the law. Without any of that, he never would have met Claire at all, so he was glad he had walked into that bank intending to rob it. He wouldn't turn the clock back, even if he could.

"Here they come," Pap said. "Reckon they'll bust down the door, and then there'll be a heap o' shootin'. You young 'uns keep your heads down."

As if that would do any good, Matt thought. He waited, holding Claire with one arm and gripping the Colt in his other hand.

Longarm leaned forward over the neck of his horse, urging the animal on to greater speed as he galloped across the plains, guided by the sound of guns in the night. The attack was going on somewhere close by, and his heart sank for a moment as he realized he was headed for the Reynolds place. The cleanup had started there. He hoped that Pap and Claire and Matt O'Hara could hold off the Hell Riders until help arrived.

A glance over his shoulder showed Longarm the dozen riders who were right behind him. Carlton Barstow hadn't wanted to help at first, saying that he didn't owe those sodbusters a damned thing, but once Longarm had explained the situation and pointed out that this was their chance to wipe out the Hell Riders, Barstow had started to come around. Longarm had added that the homesteaders would have to leave the valley anyway, since the salt deposits made the land unsuitable for successful farming, and that won Barstow over. He could afford to be generous when he was going to get what he wanted.

"That ground may not grow crops, but it'll grow enough grass for cattle!" Barstow had said as he buckled on his gun belt.

Now, with Longarm at their head, the group from the Boxed B swept over a grassy rise and came in sight of the Reynolds farm. Longarm saw the glowing hoods bobbing in the darkness and realized that this was a larger force of Hell Riders than he had seen before. Archer had sent all his hired guns after the homesteaders tonight, just as the man had said with his dying breath. Dog McCluskey and the other Hell Riders didn't know that Archer and Guinevere were dead. They were carrying out the orders they had been given.

Muzzle flashes lit up the night like a cloud of giant fireflies. The Hell Riders didn't know they were about to be under attack themselves. They outnumbered Longarm's force by more than two to one, though, so that would offset the advantage of surprise.

Unless Longarm could even up the odds a mite, right from the start.

He reached into his saddlebags and brought out one of

180

the glass killing jars he had taken from the back of Archer's wagon. He had filled it with the flammable acetate used to kill butterflies, then poked a hole in the top and wedged a piece of rag in it. Guiding his horse with his knees, Longarm struck a match and held the lucifer's flame to the makeshift fuse. It caught right away. Without wasting any time, he heaved the jar toward the Hell Riders.

It exploded like a bomb, sending flames and shards of glass spraying through the night. Several of the Hell Riders were caught in the blast. Their horses screamed and reared and toppled. The raiders' dusters were on fire, and so were the hoods they wore. The Hell Riders shrieked as real flames wreathed their heads.

Longarm lit the fuse on another jar of the liquid hellfire and flung it among the raiders as Barstow and his men opened up with their Winchesters and Colts. Their horses crashed into those of the Hell Riders. Mounts went down and men grappled hand to hand for their lives. Gun thunder filled the air, and the night sky was lit up by muzzle flashes like a lightning storm rolling across the prairie.

Longarm was in the thick of the fighting, his Colt bucking and roaring in his hand until the hammer fell on an empty chamber. He holstered it, pulled his Winchester from the saddle boot, and emptied it as well. One of the Hell Riders loomed close beside him, shouting obscene, hate-filled curses as he swung his gun toward the big lawman. Longarm lashed out one-handed with the rifle, smashing the barrel across the face of the glowing hood. The Hell Rider went backward out of his saddle, his yell cut off by the slashing hooves of another horse as it trampled him.

Before Longarm could reload, he realized that the gunshots were dying away. A couple of small fires had been started by the explosions of the killing jars, and some of Barstow's men were stamping them out. By the light of those blazes, Longarm saw that all the Hell Riders were down. A few were wounded and crying out in pain, but most of them lay in the still silence of death. A few of the Boxed B hands had been killed or wounded, too, but most of the punchers seemed to be all right.

Barstow rode over to Longarm. Blood dripped down the cattleman's fierce old face from a bullet scratch on his forehead. "Those bastards are done for," he said. "Didn't know you were carryin' bombs around with you, Long, or I might not've rode so close to you!"

Longarm didn't take the time to explain about the killing jars. He rode toward the soddy instead, with Barstow trailing behind him.

The door swung open as he reined to a halt in front of it. Pap limped out, using his rifle for a crutch. Blood stained one leg of his trousers. Claire and Matt followed him, their arms around each other.

"You folks all right?" Longarm asked them.

"Yeah, we will be, thanks to you, Marshal," Pap said. He looked past Longarm. "Barstow! That you?"

"It's me, all right, you old coot," Barstow said. "And you ought to be thankin' *me*, too. If it wasn't for me and my men, you'd be dead now, more'n likely."

Longarm nodded as he began reloading his Colt. "Barstow's right, Pap. I rode over to the Boxed B and asked him to help me wipe out the Hell Riders before they could wipe out all you homesteaders."

"You did that?" Pap asked, staring at Barstow. When the cattleman nodded, the old-timer went on, "I reckon we're obliged to you, then. But that don't mean we're gettin' off our claim."

"Oh, you'll be gettin' off of it," Barstow said with a satisfied chuckle. "No reason for you to stay. You can't grow crops here. The ground's full o' salt!"

"What!" Pap looked at Longarm. "Is this varmint tellin' the truth?"

"He is," Longarm said with a nod. "But I'm not sure you'll have to leave."

"What the hell!" Barstow blustered. "But you said—"

"I've been thinking about it," Longarm said with a grin. He holstered his Colt and kept talking.

Before he was finished, Barstow had ridden off, cussing and shaking his head.

Marshal Tom Reeder stood in front of the bar in the Double Diamond and said, "There's really that much money in salt?"

Longarm lowered his beer mug, feeling the slight pull from the bandage on his side that covered the bullet crease. He had just finished the last beer he was going to drink before he left Greenwood and started back to Denver. He set the empty mug on the bar and said, "Oh, it ain't like they found gold or anything, but the deposits in the valley are valuable enough so that those homesteaders will make more money as salt miners than they ever would have as farmers. That's why Archer was after it in the first place."

"So they're keepin' their claims anyway, and Carlton Barstow still don't get that range back?"

Longarm smiled. "That's about the size of it. But Barstow's hired himself a geologist, and he's liable to find out that he's got enough salt on the Boxed B to make a pretty nice profit from it, too."

"And you got the Dog, which is why you came here in the first place."

Longarm nodded. "Yeah, and it's a mighty good thing he had that tail. Might not've been able to identify his mangy carcass otherwise, as bad as it was burned." McCluskey had been one of the men caught in the blast of the first killing jar, and the fire had done extensive damage to his body. Longarm leaned a hip against the bar and went on, "You know, it ain't often I track down and kill an outlaw without ever saying a word to him. Fact is, Mc-Cluskey probably never knew who I was or even that a lawman had caught up to him."

"Yeah, but he's just as dead either way," Reeder pointed out.

Longarm nodded. "Yep. He won't hold up any more stagecoaches or mess with the U.S. mail. My boss can file that case away."

A step sounded behind them, and Reeder glanced over his shoulder to say, "Oh, howdy, Chad. What brings you over this way?"

Longarm looked around and saw a burly, barrel-chested man with a star pinned to his vest. The newcomer rumbled, "I'm on my way to a settlement over by the Colorado line. Got word some horse thieves who're wanted in my town are bein' held over there. Thought I'd stop off here to cut the trail dust."

"It's good to see you again," Reeder said. "Marshal, meet Chad Haimes. He's a marshal, too, only the local type, like me. Chad, this is Custis Long, deputy U.S. marshal out of Denver."

"Federal man, eh?" Haimes shook hands with Longarm. "Glad to meet you, Long." As he signaled the bartender to bring him a beer, Haimes went on, "Say, you fellas haven't seen an hombre named Matt O'Hara around these parts, have you?"

Longarm and Reeder exchanged a quick glance, and Reeder asked, "Is he a fugitive you're after, Chad?"

"O'Hara? A fugitive? Hell, no. Leastways not if he pays the twenty-five dollar fine for disturbin' the peace that the judge gave him in absentia, as they say." Haimes chuckled. "He busted our local banker in the mouth and that old sour-puss wanted him charged with attempted murder, but the judge wouldn't go along with it. I think he was like just about everybody else in town. He liked seein' Josiah Phelps with a swollen lip."

"That's all O'Hara did?" Longarm asked. "Punched a banker?"

Haimes waved a hand. "Oh, I reckon he tried to rob the bank, too, but he made such a mess of things it didn't seem worthwhile to charge him for it, especially considerin' the circumstances. Phelps was gonna be Matt's father-in-law, but his daughter broke the engagement and Phelps tried to squeeze the youngster off his ranch. You ask me, it was a stroke of luck for Matt that Abigail Phelps decided not to marry him. She's gonna make some man plumb miserable."

"This fella O'Hara shoot anybody?" Longarm asked.

"Nope. His gun went off when he was runnin' away, but the bullet went in the floor. The teller, Harvey Lapreste, squalled like he'd been shot, but the slug didn't come anywhere near him. Harvey'd just tripped over his own two feet, that's all." Haimes laughed again. "It was what you call your comedy of errors, I reckon. But Matt ran off and never came back, and I thought I'd ask about him while I was over here on this other errand. He can come back to town any time he wants to."

"Well, if I ever run into him, I'll be sure and tell him that," Reeder promised.

Haimes took a long swallow of his beer and then said to Longarm, "I reckon that ain't the way you federal boys do things, Marshal. You wouldn't ever bend the law and let a fella go just because he didn't really mean any harm."

"No, never," Longarm said with a solemn shake of his head, thinking that he would stop by the Reynolds place on his way west to let Matt know he could stop worrying about being a fugitive and concentrate on marrying Claire and making her happy. "Everything strictly by the book, that's me."

Watch for

**LONGARM AND THE
GHOST OF BLACK MESA**

the 346th novel in the exciting LONGARM
series from Jove

Coming in September!

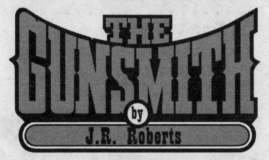

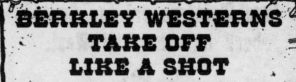